Creation I – Tales of Goodly Might

Welcome to Creation I – Tales of Goodly Might! This anthology comprises stories. The focus is on the heroes who serve the Gods of Creation, or Good. This is how the stories align with the Forsaken Isle's timeline.

- The Healer's Making is set 3,500 years before Dar Tania 1, and 5,200 years before Malcor's Story
- The Temple of the Golden Serpent is set 6 years after Malcor's Story
- The Blue Sun Staff is concurrent to Bomoki's Gate, or 1 year after Malcor's Story
- Everday Angels is set 6 years after Malcor's Story

Look for these other great titles!

Dar Tania – October 2016; read this first!
Malcor's Story – November 2016, 400+ pages
Bomoki's Gate – April 2017, 550+ pages
Dar Tania II: Set's Dream – August 2017, 250+ pages
Khalla's Play: Merakor I – January 2018, 487 pages

For more information about the stories set in the Forsaken Isles, its characters, author, or whatever else inspires you to contact me at:
www.forsakenisles.com or www.facebook.com/forsakenisles

Join my newsletter while there. If you enjoy the story, please leave a review on Amazon and Good Reads; thank you!

Edited by Ben Duffy and Tony Reynolds

ISBN: 978-0-9992552-8-5

Table of Contents

ERIC K. BARNUM

CREATION
THE HEALER'S MAKING

Creation – The Healer's Making

On the fifth day, I remember staggering into a muddy pool of water. Rain had finally come to the parched desolation of our war. We had no water. Well, we had water at the beginning, but it was targeted and destroyed until neither side had water. The lash of the whip and the screech of summoned monsters and I wondered: if they can summon demons, why not water as well?

I knelt there and longed to drink it. My fevered throat, sore from yelling, could taste it along with the iron bite of blood that colored the water a sick brown and purple mess. At that point, I would not have minded the mud. The corpses spoiling the water though, those I minded. I swore to myself I would survive. I swore to the Heavens that if I could be granted strength to endure, I would change my life, my everything.

An arrow sloshed into the muck just ahead of me. Like the rain, I barely noticed it. The arrows had flown furiously in the first two days. Now, they only fell when an archer recovered one from a body and happened to have a functioning bow. Someone, somewhere out there, had seen me and made me their enemy. I turned my head, my oaths forgotten. The red mist of rage, the curse of this war and its dark god, began to squeeze my soul in an iron grip. Kargoth, the god of fury and war, would not let me go. He had not let anyone go in this evil conflict.

With a scream rushing past my raw vocal cords, I rose up and turned in the direction of the arrow's source. A lone archer stood on a faint rise: a hill. Of earth or of bodies, I could not tell. The sun was breaking clouds behind my assailant. A murder of crows rose up between my quarry and me. He had another arrow.

The god of war mocked him. The ridicule suggested to me that even in the unlikely event it hit me, my strong armor and stalwart heart would carry me on the wings of angels to slay any opposing me. This archer was a pissant. He was already dead by my hand and had yet to realize it.

As he drew back his string and sighted it at me, I swear our eyes met. And, I saw the same god of war who was claiming a rich bounty of souls, greedily clutching at mine, also held his. I ran in Kargoth's right hand. The archer stood in the god's left hand. Like a thunderclap, we would be slammed together.

His arrow loosed and I knew it would miss. I felt invisible strings yank me aside; I was a puppet. "No!" I yelled. I wanted to die. I wanted it to be over. The only drink in my mouth was blood, my blood, from biting my lip in moments of life and death like this. It did not slake my thirst. It did not make me reconsider my reckless path. This scar around my mouth is from biting through my own face in that eternal conflict. Just a few days, but it felt like an eternity in hell. I have seen hell on Tehra; it is war.

I charged the remaining twenty paces to my foe. He seemed calm, resigned. No doubt the puppetmaster's other hand held the archer. He probably felt the strings pulling him into my sword. Where I knew I was indestructible, he knew he was doomed to die at my hand now. The fury in his eyes, the sense of betrayal made Kargoth laugh mockingly. The laugh burst from my bloody mouth and I mocked my foe.

The battlefield made movement difficult with human forms and broken armor twisted and tangled amid discarded weapons. Devils scampered about the dead feeding on flesh and killing those not yet claimed to Kargoth. They tried to trip me, but so absolute was my faith in the god of war that I did not stumble. I closed the distance easily.

My great sword, notched and chipped, earned a new impact strike as I took the archer's head. My arms were heavy and I swung them with the sword like wet sacks of dirt. Like my other kills the past few days, dehydration made his blood color wrong. His heart had stopped before I took his life. I knew this because his blood barely oozed from the stump of his neck. Mad thoughts returned to me... urging me to drink the blood. This time, I could not deny the thirst demons and I fell on the archer.

When I regained my senses, I discovered the bounty at my feet. Somehow, my foe had recovered a quiver of arrows. I counted eight. The bow had to be enchanted, though I could not tell because of grime and dirt. The silver string alone made me think it magic. Shaking from exhaustion – the god only let us sleep when our unconscious minds would no longer obey orders to fight – I placed an arrow on the bow and looked for an enemy.

I could not remember which side of the battlefield I had begun on. I could not remember what my banner, what my lord, what my master-at-arms looked like. Everything was earthen paint clumped together by the life fluids of once living men. I looked for hours, my legs unwilling to move. When I saw nothing, the war god let me go and went to find another puppet to control. He reassured me that soon enough I would take another harvest.

I fell to my knees and found the archer's name: Sir Cuthiel di Longmel. It was a good name. I recognized it as my enemy. The Longmels had allied with the Drow rather than choosing to fight against them. The cost of the alliance was they gave up their children, younger than fourteen, to the Drow. The elderly were dismissed as refugees. The rest were armed and sent to march on the fiefdoms resisting the Drow all around the Longmel borderlands.

The Longmels were evil to ally with the Drow. Of course, they had heard the stories I lived through. Yes, I lived... while my community died. We did not face dark elves. We faced a mad garrison of once-holy knights convinced we had converted to Lolth's worship. They burned my village and began indiscriminately killing everyone. I survived because, well, I was a knight of the Sun God. Maybe they let me be, thinking I was one of them. Maybe the Sun God wanted me to see how twisted my fellow knights had become. I like to think that even then in my darkest moments of wallowing despair and suicidal slavishness to Kargoth, my true self was desperately looking for redemption.

No, I need to correct this. I *was* a knight of the Sun God before those knights came. It was not the Sun God that killed my family and friends. It was madness. It was Lolth. It was the Drow. I tore my mantle. I anointed my holy sword in the blood of my family and pledged revenge. That was when Kargoth, the War Lord, offered me a new way. I at last understood how a paladin falls.

I don't remember my name. I remember battle lust, so much rage, burning in my heart. It felt holy and sanctifying at first, but when it overflowed my soul and lit my body afire with power, I knew its source: warp and hell.

The War Lord let me go for a time after I killed the archer. Maybe he enjoyed my lucid moments of self-loathing and regret as much as he enjoyed the blade offerings I sent him. Sir Cuthiel di Longmel. It was a good name. His murder marked what I now understand as my first step back towards the light.

Knowing my time as myself was short, I prayed to the Sun God. I knew there would be no answer. I had no atonement. How could I? My mission was not complete and soon Kargoth would reattach those puppet strings.

So that it would be my revenge, my vengeance, I stripped Cuthiel and donned his clothing, his emblems. I took his bow. The sun was dripping below the setting horizon. Rain clouds moving towards me came alive with color. Then, the storm cut off my color sight and returned my world to twilight grays. That told me where West lay. The Longmels were north. In disguise, I marched north.

Only a handful of Longmels survived. They hailed me and I waved wearily as I trudged past them. Several drank from a barrel collecting rain water. I needed a drink before Kargoth made me his avatar again. I knew he laughed at me. He reveled at my dark plan but let me drink first.

The water was sweet but my hands shook in twilight as I murdered the three fighters at the barrel. No one heard. They were dead anyway.

Not the king, but someone important had survived to rally what remained. A war wizard stood next to him with two other fighters. The wizard was spent. To appear so shabby, he would not even spare a spell to clean himself. Merakor, as it had been, would laugh to see a wizard so broken and bent.

I looked down so they would not see the mad light in my eyes. But, my soul screamed out with each step like a drum's cadence, *Kargoth! Kargoth!*

I sheathed my sword in the mage's back, stabbing down into his pelvis and thighs. The three fighters jumped back into defensive positions. One ran. That left just two and I saw Kargoth take hold of the noble born son of Longmel. I dropped the bow and quiver by the mage's body and said, "Hold these for me." The puppetmaster wanted me calm.

I wanted to call for a truce, for an end to the war. Instead, I attacked. Longmel counter-attacked. With no care to defend, we brutalized each other. Our blades slid along the other's until our hilt guards locked. The grim satisfaction in Longmel's eyes was haunting. Rather than lock and struggle, I dropped to the ground and kicked sideways.

My kick stumbled Longmel into his friend. But, I did not stop my movement with a mere kick. Strengthened by Kargoth, I splashed mud into their faces. I meant to kill Longmel, but my sword saved him for last. It did not surprise me. Kargoth always fought from weakest to strongest. Many of my wounds were because I allowed myself to be flanked by the strongest as I demoralized them by slaying their friends, their families, and their allies.

Longmel overhead chopped down onto me as I yanked my sword out of the lungs and armor of his friend. I did not flinch. I should have flinched. My armor held and I laughed saying, "You don't even understand. You never will, Longmel." My counterattack drove my blade up into his helmet visor.

With mud spilling into my armor and my victim leaning down into me, I put my foot against his chest and kicked him to the side. My sword screeched out of his helmet. "Kargoth!" I shouted.

Only night and heavy rain answered me. But, I remember screaming the god's name over and over again until my own darkness took me.

I don't know how long I slept. When I finally woke, I was burning with fever. The sun was out. The barrel was full of fresh water. Carrion birds and devils crawled the battlefield. I was alone except for the shrieking of the wounded as demons devoured them.

I drank and drank until I could drink not a single drop more. In the quietude of the hellacious charnel house, I caught my own reflection, and then vomited.

You see, I was hideous with evil. I did not recognize myself. I looked drunk with murder. By the trembling in my eyes and hands, I knew I craved more death until at last I would find my own.

What is, what was my name? I still don't know.

Here is what I do know: I was drunk with death and yet craved more. I had become an ugly thing and I hated myself. I took my sword and began to plan my own end. I prayed to Pha Rann, but my voice choked. I could not sully the Bright God's name with my suicide. The war god laughed at me. "The world is full of life. Your harvest is not yet done," his laughter seared into my thoughts. "The world is ripe with living who must die."

With my sword resting against the bottom of my jaw, all I had to do was let my body weight drive it into my brain. "You will rise as my revenant, fool. No, you will take this fight to the Drow. They are your real enemy anyway."

The Drow! My hands began to tremble. This was an eternity ago and yet, look! Telling this story makes them tremble still. I do not know if my faith in Braden would allow me to endure confrontation with the Drow. The Tanian lord, Daryx, he avoids me but sent word once. He offered to test me and see, for my own assurance. I do not trust myself and so avoid the Lord Daryx.

Back to the past wars… so, I nodded and took my sword from my own neck. I took the bow, and arrows and began hunting for the tools I would need. The Longmel battlefield became my gruesome armory. The dead rose up and offered me their best armor, their best swords. In an hour, I was adorned with enchanted everything. The Drow must be harvested… for Kargoth. As I turned to march on the Elven Triopolis, the dead followed me. You would think they would be zombies, but so empowered by Kargoth were they that they loped ahead and all around me like swarming cockroaches.

No, I never found actual Drow. The hallmark and legend of this war was how effectively they twisted Merakor against itself. When a people are blessed as were the Korans, when they turn away from the Sun, their darkness is beyond a simple shadow. The Drow did not need to fight me. They sent my fellow Korans against my undead army.

At some point, I do not know how long, my slaughter path led me to a place where I could not continue. My undead had long ago fallen to clerics and others. Or, I ended them myself.

I found a small village of elves. They were scared. Somehow the war had raged past them, like waves breaking around a sand bar. A young girl's eyes dilated at the tip of my sword as I trembled wanting to kill her, wanting to save her.

Can I be redeemed? I did not know. The first decent thing I ever did was resist Kargoth's claim of the girl as a sacrifice. I was locked, unable to move, unable to breathe lest I lose my control to the puppetmaster. I was that tired of slaying. Kargoth laughed at me and assured me that these refugees would all fall to my blade. He tried to twist my thoughts to show them as Drow. But, I was so tired of my not-alive not-dead war that I choked back and willed that Kargoth let me die or kill me. Take my soul and be done, I remember howling at the war god in my dark prayers.

The mother begged and cried at my feet. When anyone attempted to move the child, my sword followed. I was a frozen reaper, ready to strike but somehow unable to. They could not separate my blade from the hand's distance away from the girl's eyes.

The girl's fear changed to curiosity faster than I could believe, than I can still believe. She said, "What's your name?"

I sputtered. I could not remember my name, any more than I can now.

"I am not a Drow, sir," the girl pled. "They killed my daddy though no one believed me. Did the Drow kill your daddy?"

I nodded and felt a puppet string break. "What is your name?" I asked. I know that my face, my eyes, my countenance radiated murder, but I nearly wept to hear myself ask a congenial question. Mercy began to break more puppet strings. I saw and hated myself, but unlike the rage that filled my own self-realizations, I finally felt acceptance. Not for being a murderer, but acceptance that my sacrifice to Kargoth had been misguided.

The mother was still pleading, "No, no, no..."

"It's okay, mommy. The Drow took his family too. Maybe he's just confused, like the others." Another string broke. The girl said, "My name is Vel Spren. If you kill me, it will not bring your family back. You must carry a heavy burden. So many dead, everywhere. Please, do not let this become another burden. Your soul is breaking to pieces. I can see it."

The last Kargoth string broke and I let go of my sword and fell to my hands and knees before her. Vel Spren cradled my face in her hands. I did not ask for it. But, she said, "I forgive you."

I remember being offended at the notion that I needed forgiveness. I was already beyond it. Hell had taken me and would never let go. Yet, in her words, when I fought back the puppet strings trying to reattach at my supposed offense, I found a glimmering vein of hope. Of course, I knew not that this girl child was a member of the Royal Family of Vel, rulers of the Triopolis. After her brother, Vel Pajor, she wold be next in line for the throne. I know this now. It's funny what I do and do not remember. It is a blessed mercy from Braden that I cannot remember everything. I suspect my afterlife will require atonement for the things I do not remember now.

"Vel Spren, I do not remember my name. My soul is broken, like our empire." I felt a tear well up in my eye. Once it started I could not stop it. I wept for Merakor, for Vel Spren's father, for my wife, for Merakor, and for my own soul.

Vel Spren sat by me and patted my hand. Her touch burned. The elves adopted me like a sick fetish for a time, which I later learned was five years. Anytime an enemy scout came and found our encampment, their death happened quickly. The elves did not even see it. Vel Spren's mother told me I would stand and walk towards an enemy long before the elves even knew. Our enemies recognized me as a death knight. They would hail me and I would call back to them. There would be a red mist and the ending of sounds. After, they would find body parts and broken trees across an arc of thirty paces. Within a year, there was a perimeter around the camp of broken trees. My defense was marking our location.

I do not remember how many times that happened before my tears ceased. When I was all cried out, and in a quiet moment, I realized I must never touch a weapon again. I removed my armor. I dropped my weapons, all of them. The enchanted rings and tokens all came off until I was naked. The elves would not touch them, believing them cursed.

My body, as you see, is mostly scars. I washed myself in a waterfall's pool. Vel Spren told me the water ran with foul smells and blood for hours while I washed. The cold water cleansed not just my flesh, but my soul. I remember seeing things differently. The parts of myself I could not recognize washed away and with them.

When I came out, my hair was white. My eyes were white. A symbol burned in my mind and when I prayed to any god, I only heard this:

> *You must heal the world.*

> I asked, "Who are you? May I know the name of the god that would heal the world?"

> *My name is Braden. You must heal the world. Will you?*

> I called out, "Yes, I will heal the world."

> *Heal the world.*

> "What must I do?"

> *Heal our world.*

That is all I ever hear now when I pray to Braden.

The elves did not know this god. I had never heard of a Braden. After Kargoth, I was loath to pledge myself to an unknown god. In my doubts, Braden spoke more to me, more than at any other time since.

He said:

> *While I am unknown, you will know what you must do. You judge whether I be evil or good. But, know this: the way of the sword is no longer your path. I have purchased your soul from Kargoth and Hell. The world needs you. It is the time of healing. You will see that*

ideas and gentle mercies can be just as powerful as a sword. Your role is to save, to guide, to cherish.

* * *

When I looked at Vel Spren, I saw what she had hidden from me all this time – she was terrified of me. She felt that by giving herself to me, I would not kill her mother. She had resigned herself to becoming my slave in all ways, even if it meant giving me her most precious self and being with me as child-wife. It hurt me to see this. Her mother was no different. I could see her conflict: they wanted me dead or gone or both, but they had no fighters. The mother was resigned to give herself to me to save the community, and to save Vel Spren.

When the community of survivors came to me, I saw a similar fearful compromise in their hearts. Vel Spren was noble and each had committed to offering themselves to me to save Vel.

I raised my hands and said, "Blessed be you, remnants of Vel. Braden, the god of healing, is here with you. You are cherished. The god of war is gone from me. In his name, I bless you."

My words! I remember how weak they felt. You can only imagine my surprise when white light pulsed from my heart and like chain lightning struck the hearts of the elves. In a single heartbeat, they knew what I had been told. They knew I had become safe for them.

Vel Spren cried first and ran to my arms. We embraced and for the first time since I bade my dead family good-bye, I felt the true love of another mortal being. "You are safe, Vel Spren."

"I know," she whispered into my neck and hugged me even tighter.

Like the wind before a storm, Vel Spren's hug brought more and more of the elves to me until we all hugged and Braden's peace warmed us. Like the wind before a storm, we knew this would not last long. Scouts had been increasing in frequency. A storm of war would soon hit this tiny island of peace. "We need to leave. Braden will guide us," I said. It was a perfectly quiet moment.

"Where to?" Vel Spren asked. I guess the community had made her the spokesperson with me. I did not realize it before my consecration to Braden.

Oh, what happened to her?, you ask. No, she did not make it to the Exodus. That is another story, but she gave herself for me. I did not want her to, but Braden works in strange ways. Her sacrifice sorely tested my resolve to never pick up another weapon, or take a life. I passed my test and did not forsake my vows to Braden.

Yes, she died, but her sacrifice saved thousands and inspired tens of thousands more. You might know her now by her legend – the Silvespren Dragon? Yes, yes. Many think Silvespren is a corruption of the silver dragon-type. That is not the case. She chose to serve the All-Father and drew an army after her when she became a silver dragon.

Oh, she was glorious! She rather reminds me of the Tanian dragons. Except that where the Tanians are dreadful and heavy in their might, Silvespren was bright. The All-Father knew we needed a miracle and gave us Silvespren. She took on an entire army to save us.

Here is the only thing I call my own. This medallion is Braden's symbol on a silver dragon scale. Dear Vel Spren gave this to me and told me to tell her story. To tell you: a life served for all is the only life with meaning, is the only service worth serving for.

I'm an old man. What else would you like to know? Soon, the wind will urge me to leave and I must follow it. Already, the Valley of Bloodstone cries out for healing. For now, I am here. So, bring your sick, your maimed, and your cursed to me. They hear my call, but may be unable to move, or resisting because they are held back by evil vanity. Bring them to me.

Oh? Silvespren. That is my favorite story. Let me tell you though it takes a while to build to the Silver Dragon you call Silvespren.

* * *

She was young, even for an elf. She was thirty-three. In human terms, that would make her maybe twelve or thirteen. She was a gray elf, you know, the ones most gifted with magic and divine powers. She was the niece of the king in Havkor, Vel Pajor's father. Let's see, she had silver-white hair and a faint gray countenance set in a perfectly smooth complexion. Unlike the elves that survived the Exodus, Vel Spren had an air of eternal youthfulness and hope so bright it could mask the stars.

When we left the refuge, the elves trailed me. They were concerned I did not don my armor and weapons, but with faith in me and this unknown god, they followed. I saw them hesitate to pick up my many tokens of war and I cautioned them. I have no doubt they are cursed, probably still.

We marched east. Always east. I would stop when Braden told me to stop. Sometimes we would stay in place for days, only to find that some army had passed us in the night. I prayed things would continue this way.

As we went, we encountered refugees who joined us. We had been moving slowly this way, and with ever growing numbers, when word reached me that we had run out of food. Our camp had grown so large I could not see the starvation. I remember walking into a once verdant cropland, now burned and soiled by years of fighting. What were once scarecrows now held crucified bodies posed as trophies in some long-ago battle.

In my eyes, the wrongness inflicted by brother on brother here made my heart ache. I know that I left many a town a harvest of carnage just like this. I pushed that recollection out of my thoughts and knelt. My hands on the ground felt right. *This is what Braden wants me to do*, I thought. I prayed, and not just for the wrong to be righted, but for the refugees with me. I prayed for their continuing safety, for their need for food, and for the sorrow we beheld. The sorrow was not just here, it was strewn about our meandering eastward path.

From my fingers, I felt vitality flow into the soil. I felt roots push against my hands and then, like a child unsure where to run, springtime came to the field in a rush of green. Flowers burst and then ripened to fruit and corn. Long dormant seeds welcomed us and hurried to mature. My camp burst into applause and my heart ached for their want and need. That they saw this as food rather than a miraculous blessing hurt, but I understood.

Vel Spren patted my shoulder and said, "Braden gives us treasure we do not deserve."

I nodded. "Such is the way of Braden. To heal the world, we must tend to the world's garden keepers."

Vel Spren turned to the group and began to speak. Somehow, she said the words I knew needed to be said. I will never forget. These are her words, forever locked in my heart:

"Survivors of Merakor, hear me! You are hungry and tired and scared. This is how evil wants you to feel. This is how fear grows. It thrives in the darkness of our despair. The miracle before us is not one of food. It is a sign that we are to take hope, keep our faith in Braden and the Sun God. We are on the right path. Nothing will defeat us. Our enemies would have us starve, or turn on one another. If we take this blessing as an entitlement, we cheapen Braden's gift. If we accept this as yet another sign that Braden's Nameless Priest is our savior, we cheapen each and every step we make east. We walk by faith. We walk in the light of Pha Rann, guided by the god Braden. While we might rejoice in this miracle, let us take note of the blight in this place and give heed to the suffering and broken hearts shattered here. While we might be tempted to praise Braden, let us instead join our prayers to Braden's Priest and pray for this land and those who fell here."

When the bursting plants reached the scarecrows on which impaled skeletons hung, flesh rose up on the dead bodies and three women fell to the ground. One was an elf. The other two were humans. The looked around in disbelief and then cautiously approached us. Vel Spren took them clothing and my camp offered them food and drink.

Against the wrack and ruin all around, our blossomed field would draw attention. I knew it even without Braden telling me a trial was coming.

The trial took two days to arrive. In that time, we learned the story of the three women. They were druids, sacrificed by their once prosperous town as a sign to the Drow that they had chosen to serve Lolth rather than fight for Merakor. We were in Talkra, the eastern farmland that once produced most of the staple crops for Merakor. They warned us to avoid it. They said, "It is possessed by ghosts and worse. The Drow summoned demons, titanic demons, who hunt day and night for survivors not marked by Lolth."

In that moment, I knew what my trial would be. It began that night with the voice of a child crying in the distance.

I could not sleep that night, not that I ever really sleep anymore. I sit quietly and ponder always where Braden would have me be. I arose and walked west through the camp, in the direction of the child's cries. We must have grown to thousands from the original two hundred elves. At the westward edge, I found everyone asleep. So absolute was their trust in me through countless near misses that they slept without sentries.

I heard the child crying again. This time, my ears could tell it was not a child, but a demon in the shape of a child. I touched the old men and younger women on guard. They startled awake and clutched at what weapons they had. Perhaps sensing something amiss, the three druids joined me.

The druids' leader, the elf whose name I do not remember, said, "We are ready to fight, my lord."

I touched her shoulder and shook my head. "Fighting will lead to more fighting. This is not my way. You have seen where this path takes you. If you are to come with me, to stay with us, you must forsake fighting and give your faith over to Braden."

They had heard this from the other refugees. I knew they had. But hearing me say it, seeing me walk into the darkness unarmed and unafraid, the elf said, "You're mad."

I remember laughing and said, "No, you are mad to continue repeating the path of war. That path leads only to death and more death multiplied. Trust in me if not Braden."

They came with me. We found a small girl child. She had blood and wounds all over her. She looked up from red eyes and a runny nose. She began to whimper but I held up my hand. "Good evening servant of evil," I said.

The girl looked at me wide-eyed and then looked all around, still trying to play the part of a small girl. "Where?" she jumped up and ran towards me for succor.

I felt the druids tense and signaled them to do nothing. The girl demon got within five steps of me before a blast of radiant light stopped her in her tracks as if she had run into a wall. So massive was the actual creature in the girl's form that the ground trembled when she fell back to her bottom.

"Please, I'm scared," she said.

I shook my head. "You are not a girl and you are not welcome in this world. You are dismissed."

The girl began to laugh at me. "Idiot! Fool!" she screamed. "To think a nobody like you..."

A black gate opened at my words behind her and clawing tendrils of ink blackness reached for her, for it. I pointed to it. "The world is ill with your unnaturalness. Begone."

The girl saw the gate. "No! How? We had a deal..." she screamed as she tried to run away. Each tendril pulled part of her back into the gate and like a pie being eaten, she vanished in clawed bites. I sensed more of the creatures approaching from the west.

I felt a measure of balance restored to this place with the creature's banishment. But more were coming.

"I don't believe it," the druid elf said.

"Yet you must. Braden's purpose is to heal the world. More of these wolves in human form are coming."

An hour passed and nothing happened until at last a giant appeared, towering against the starlit sky. It jumped and landed before me. It was a red slaad, or an Embros. Imagine a red toad that stands as tall as three men and is almost as wide as it is tall with muscle. Scaled not too unlike a dragon or a serpent. It leered down at me and yet I stood unconcerned. If it killed me, I would mourn the slaughter of those who followed but Braden told me that would not happen.

I did not know that name – Embros – for a long time. Slaads are shapeshifters from the Abyss, you see. They serve Set. They are evil beyond what a mortal understands of evil. I tell you this so you can know and grow in knowledge that, while good and evil exist on a spectrum in our world, those concepts each have their spectrums and evil, as a human sees it, is just an iota of what Set's evil truly is. To comprehend it, you must somehow remove yourself from an understanding of morality and embrace only the totality of hungry malice that is Set.

"I dare you to abjure me too, mage," the Embros said through drool. "You see my true form and know you cannot endure or compel the mighty Neeralyx."

"I am not a mage. Your name means nothing to me. You are a disease on this land. I would cure you," I said.

The Embros flexed its muscles and sniffed the air. "How is it that you have so much food with you?" Neeralyx demanded of me. "Crops? Drinks? Thousands of heart beats. I cleansed this land…" The slaad's voice trailed away as its eyes fixated on the druids. "Ah, you three. So the witches of Talkra survived!" It began to laugh. From behind it, ten of these demons walked into our field of view.

Look at my arm, my hair stands on end remembering it. I was so caught up in Braden during that time I did not consider the enemies I faced.

A smaller blue-tinged Slaad walked forward and stood at the Embro's side. As it did, its form shifted into a human male… and I understood. "No," I said. "Your masters would have you twist us upon ourselves like a starving snake. I am here to unravel the knots you have made of this land and its people. You may not take the form of any of those here again." I turned to the druids and explained, "They have some ability to know us, either by desire or memory, and they use the shapes of those we care about to spread lies and poison."

At my words, the blue toad's form melted back into blue… and then faded to an unhealthy green. With each step, I found knowledge entering me. They have a true form but prefer other stronger or more attractive forms. They are full of self-loathing. "You masquerade in higher forms than even your master allows. That might work against the uninformed but I see you as you are."

I pointed at Neeralyx. "You are real, but your army is weak." I pointed to the once blue, now green toad-man. "And you are full of lies. I would end the charade now."

The Embros eyed me, now more warily. "You have power. I must have it."

"If you harm me, you will regret it," I said.

Neeralyx straightened his spine to look down at me from the height of four men now. "You threaten me."

"Take it how you wish."

The green toad-men attacked me. I said to the druids, "Do not raise your weapons. We stand with faith." The druids nodded but I could feel their anxiety.

The green slaads slammed into my divine protection, same as the little girl had. Driven by the Embros, they recovered their footing and tried again. One had come into possession of magic and he struck at me with an enchanted blade. In years, I had not been wounded in a way I could feel. It surprised me when the blade cut into my stomach. The druids screamed but I felt knowledge instead of pain. I understood the cut, how it disrupted my natural organization, and how it might be healed with and without divine aid. The slaad looked at me triumphantly and drove the sword through my torso.

"I feel nothing," I said. The slaad began screaming in agony. It fell back from me as blood rushed from its front and back mid-section. In moments, it was dead. The other slaads shrank away. The Embros growled and focused its eyes on me as I pulled the cursed weapon out of my body. It did not even leave blood. "A golden sword?" I noted.

"Touch me," I said to the druids. I did not know what it was then, but Set's Dream washed over us and tried to alter our world. I felt the curse begin reaching towards the camp. "No, Neeralyx. Your curse ends tonight."

It blinked at me in shock as its power ended. "You see what happens to those that attack me. You see what power stands against you. I give you this choice: leave, or repent."

Neeralyx laughed. "Leaving is no choice. You make demands you lack power to enforce. My armies already encircle your valley of food."

"You lie. In fact, you are trying to escape the Drow. I can tell you are being hunted and fear for your life. Another one like you but beholden to another hunts you right now." I pointed to one of the green toad-men. "That one's master."

Neeralyx's eyes dilated and he swung to the side as the green one's form erupted and spilled out another Embros, already attacking.

My memories of what happened next are still jumbled in my mind. Somehow Neeralyx decided to use me as a shield, and Braden let it happen. Neeralyx swung me like a buckler. Braden's barrier blasted this other Embros time and again. As evil as they are, even now, I find some measure of admiration for a creature able to adapt. After all, I had stripped Neeralyx of all its primary weapons.

When the battle was over, only Neeralyx remained. "What are you?" it asked. The slaad kept flexing its mouth clearly wanting to bite my head. Unanswered, Neeralyx tore into the other red's head and ate the brain. I could tell this had some effect on it though it seemed a strange ritual to me in the moment. Of course, we know now that a Slaad can obtain memories and knowledge through consumption like this. It's one of their greatest weapons against us.

"What are you?" Neeralyx screamed at me. "How could you know this? What is your name? Are you Polgeryx? Show yourself to me!"

"I do not know what a Polgeryx is. My god shows me all that is wrong in the world. For some reason, I am not enjoined to abjure you back to the Abyss. I wonder why."

"Because you are weak, human fool." The Embros grabbed me and shook me as hard as he could. I felt nothing. The druids had relaxed and seemed to enjoy the slaad's frustration.

It made Neeralyx angry, even as I saw vertigo began to affect the Emros from its shaking me. It turned to slash its tail at the druids. All three of them were smashed back and down into the dirt. After the nothing at all I felt from being attacked, the violence and destruction of that one attack and how it killed the three druids taught me something: while I am protected, those with me are not, at least not in the same way. "How could you know Polgeryx seeks me?!" It's scream echoed all around us. Later, Vel Spren told me they almost rushed to our aid. The terrible screams and my explicit orders alone gave them pause.

I felt indignation. Had I banished this beast, the druids would not have died. The slaad threw me down. I easily recovered my feet even though the force of the throw cratered the ground. "I wonder," it growled at me. "If I eat your head, would you survive?"

I ignored it and walked to the three ladies. Neeralyx did not like being casually disregarded. As I walked, he tried to bite my head. Like the girl child that attacked me, a divine barrier threw the slaad back from me. I turned my head and noted that its long fangs had broken. It howled and continued bellowing loud pain while I resurrected the three druids again.

"Please," I said. "You must exercise caution around me and our enemies. In their sickness, they do not understand the harm they do."

Behind us, Neeralyx continued screaming and its language twisted into an infernal caricature of the Koran tongue. Apparently, its teeth were supposed to regenerate but were not doing so. "I must go and tend this one. Braden has a purpose for him."

The elf druid caught my hand and shook her head, no. "Please, Nameless One, do not do this. That thing is evil. It can have no purpose but to destroy."

When I took her hand, I saw an image of the three. They had each been married. They had each had children. I could feel their love for their families. At some point, the slaads had replaced their husbands or children. Rumors of devil worship had been spread until, with the rumors of war, the people did not believe or trust the druids.

I reassured her. "I see your pain and understand the context. I know this is not what you want, but know this: your husbands…" I caught all of their attention. "They were all killed. So were your children. They have ascended to heaven. The imposters that replaced them knew they were manipulating your love. In Braden's name and light, I free you from regret and self-doubt. You did all that you could. Take what peace you can and join me, sisters. We must take this group east. I sense that by the time we reach our destination, we will many tens of thousands. Go back to the camp and ready them to march. Do not burden yourselves with food. Same as now, Braden will provide for us."

Neeralyx was holding his mouth and taking shallow breaths through the sides of his cheeks. "What did you do to me, human?!"

"I did nothing. You inflicted this evil on yourself and in spite of seeing how this played out for the others. I have a question to ask, but first let us reason: you are hunted, you are hated, and you are in over your head. Your chances of survival are nonexistent. Why not come with us?"

Neeralyx eyed me. "Join you? Why not? You will heal me?"

I touched his hand. It felt alien and slimy. "To the extent you are loyal to Braden's cause, you are healed."

Neeralyx resisted Creation's pull. "To be healed, you must let this happen, Neeralyx."

"I'm trying," he choked. "It burns."

"Yes, it is cleansing you."

I understand now that Slaads serve Set and are altogether evil beyond our ken. Yet I swear to you, in that moment, a Slaad was redeemed of Set, if not of evil. I felt something dark and festering leave the creature. Neeralyx felt it too and its eyes opened wide. "You broke the connection to my Anthracos; how?"

"I do not know what this means. But Neeralyx, this is your first step on a different path. You are in the service of Braden, who would heal – not consume – the world. Each time you are healed, Braden will make you more of his. Each time you rebel or do your own faithless thing, that healing will be rescinded. Understand this. It is not me. It is not my camp of survivors. You will lose this gift each time you betray us, because consequence is a law of heaven."

I kept my hand on the oily snake-like skin of its hand. It was warm and cold at the same time. I said, "This is your first step into an existence you have never known before. In this moment, you are free, truly free. I ask you to please, I urge you to make your first choices wisely. I am going back to camp now."

Neeralyx nodded while flicking his now-healed teeth with a long blue tongue. His form shrank until a beautiful dark elf in the garb of a paladin stood by my side. "Will this form please you?" the new female knight said.

"Your motives in this are offensive, Neeralyx. Be careful."

The sensual female form adjusted to be more functional and less titillating. Though the presence of Neera, as she chose to be called, stirred the camp, they quickly came to view her as my bodyguard. I wish I could say that Neera was redeemed. The truth is that over time, the Slaad came to view me as a prized trophy and became enraged with jealousy whenever I was targeted by an enemy. The end effect was that I had a very avid bodyguard. In hindsight, it has occurred to me that jealousy must be the closest to loyalty and love an Abyssal creature can get.

Vel Spren took to Neera quickly. The Vel family never held the dark elves in ill will until the Kinslayer Wars ended Merakor. Perhaps, like me before redemption, she hoped to win Neeralyx over as a new protector for our camp. I know it hurt her that she failed, and it was quickly apparent that redemption for a slaad is a momentary event. It still hurts me that I was unable to affect the evil in Neeralyx. Perhaps the Slaads cannot be cured of evil until Set is truly ended.

Once we had Neera, things progressed more smoothly. I hate to admit it but she used her control of Set's Dream to make us look like just another army. 'Set's Dream' was what Neera called it. Because I had banished this power from her, she could not use it against us and those in my camp, under my care. However, it worked well against those who sought to harm us. Maybe I should explain?

You know that Set is bound deep in slumber, deep in the Abyss. You know that Set desires only to consume the universe, and that all of the foul and unorganized atrocities throughout are spawned from the nightmares of Set's eternal sleep. The Slaads believe, perhaps they know that Set has the form of a dragon, titanic like the mountains, and covered in eyes. Neera believes, and I came to understand some of the truth in this, that when cataclysm and murder are rife, an eye of Set opens and watches. That single, or several eyes, grant the worshipper of Set great power. In Neera's case, she could cast an illusion that actually altered reality.

This illusion is Set's Dream. While we saw and knew us as ourselves, our enemies saw a mighty army of Drow... and gave us wide berth. I once asked Neera about this and remember he mocking answer. "Let us attack them, Nameless Priest! You will see, on this side, a small Vel Spren being herself. But, to our enemies, you might see the power of the Dream! That same Vel wreaking carnage and violent killing. May we?"

The funny thing is, and I did not know it then as I do now, this power is addictive to them. They want it. They worship it. It feeds them. Though I did not meet her, I once exchanged letters with Tania's medusa, Syliri. She explained this in more detail to me. I'm sure you have a copy of this? Yes. Then, I will continue.

The exodus progressed for months, adding to our ranks along the way. With so many indigent, old, and very young, we did not move quickly and when winter arrived, we were just on the outskirts of Talkra. Braden urged me ever eastward. The road became increasingly dire and haunted. When Braden bade me, I recovered fallen heroes and they joined our ranks. They shared with us tales of demons and haunted spirits blighting Talkra.

I remember climbing a hill and seeing on the eastern horizon the grand buildings of commerce, trade, and government. I could see them but my eyes rejected the ruin of blasted stone and smoke haze clinging to what remained of the tall towers. I could see wrongness moving its way throughout the city. Though the demons were invisible, I could see their passing in how the air currents moved around them. Every so often, they would reach down and grab something.

Neera said, "The resistance still remains. I am impressed."

Her words electrified me. This was my purpose in coming east! Vel Spren urged us forward exclaiming, "If there is a resistance, maybe we can save them and they will join us!"

Neera grinned. "With Type Nine demons, doubtful. Like I said, I'm impressed."

Vel Spren squinted at the city. "I don't see anything. What is a type nine?"

Neera patted her on the head and said, "You are so delicious, Vel. Are all children like you, or just elves? There are nine hells, right? You know this. So, why nine?"

Vel Spren gave a textbook answer, "Because Asmodei was content with nine. There are probably more but no hero has ever…"

Neera interrupted her. "There are nine, which is to say that Asmodei considered some number of the hells to be perfect. And he made the Ninth his throne to hold the Gate of Warp. So, when an archmage summons a demon with aid from Asmodei, it is therefore called a 'type nine' because… why?" I had long ago stopped noticing the patronizing tone. After all, if I were titanic compared to us, I might feel a bit condescending every once in a while. It's a size thing.

"Well, I suppose it should be a devil, but I can see by your scowl it's not." Vel Spren thought more and then said, "Because while the demons are known to the Lord of Warp, a type nine demon would be what Asmodei considers a perfect demon?"

"She gets it!" Neera mocked to me. "A devil serves Asmodei, or is bound to some purpose. A demon is either from the

Abyss, like these, or are devils let loose in this world." Neera pointed to the type nine and the hundreds of gates dotting the sky behind its massive form. "Without purpose, they engage in sport. Maybe the Drow can bind them? It's a pity you cannot see my sisters. They are beautiful, in a demonic way."

"I can see them," I said.

Neera eyed me suspiciously again. "You see and know too much, Nameless. It concerns me that a Tehran can know so many things. I can see them, for they are my sisters in the Dream."

I pointed. "Braden urges me forward. I would leave the host here. I will go alone and seek out this resistance."

Neera unclipped her sword from its scabbard. "I will go with you. I cannot risk my own ascension, Nameless, to my sisters. If you fall to them, and not to me..." she often talked this way. I share this with you because it is every Slaad's dream to encounter a powerful mortal and eat them. Neera was convinced that if she consumed me, she would ascend to Anthracos, maybe

I shrugged. "I do not care where you go, Neera. Braden has no purpose for you as of yet. And, you still make the exodus uneasy. Yes, you will come with me."

I knew Vel Spren wished to come. I embraced her. "I need you to stay here. They view you as the last remaining Vel, princess of Havkor. You are their morale and spirit. Please stay."

She stepped back and touched my chin. "Master," she said, as that's what they had started calling me. "Braden does not tell me to stay, or to go. So, I choose to come with you. The three sisters can watch over them."

The three of us left. I remember turning and see the entire camp waving at me, wishing us luck. We had grown to fill the entire valley. I had not realized it. It happened gradually, day by day as we marched. Small groups, even individual stragglers would join us. My only involvement came when Braden moved me to intercept enemies trying to join as spies. Neera had a keen sense for these as well.

Since that time, I have been in many a place where the exodus is speculated about. "Why were there no Drow?" I have heard asked. "How did the exodus remain free of spies, and other shapeshifters, even demons?"

The answer is that we had some Drow, but they were redeemed. We had some spies, but Braden allowed them to come for purposes later revealed. It still saddens me that Vel Spren and Neera did not make it. In some ways, they were my first friends. The elves remain a warm fire of love in my heart. You have no idea how it warms me to be here with you all.

* * *

I talked to the great elf archmage Galthrest about his ordeals in Talkra after the exodus. He was quite insane. Braden cannot cure that which by the person's own design is self-inflicted madness. After what he endured at the hands of demons, I cannot judge his decision to retreat into the chambers of his own mind. We are each in control of our destiny and the choice to descend into insanity is one that cannot be cured. Choices and their consequences are an intractable disease. When the madness comes from some other source, Braden is pleased to dismiss such ailments. I wish I could have been an instrument in restoring hope to Galthrest.

You see, the problem is especially pronounced in immortal races. Until I endured more years than I can remember at this point, I would not have realized it. You see, for elves like Galthrest, even like you, there is a certain joy in life… where you wake up each day and find some reason to participate in that day in the moment. All immortal races are subject to this, and I understand even the long-lived Tanian priestesses have seen this. When by boredom, by toxic regret, by suffering, the joy of each day becomes too hard to endure, then Time changes. Instead of welcoming the moment and deriving immortality from anticipation of the next and the next, you pull yourself out of Time's flow. For elves, this causes aging.

Galthrest had aged. Let me step back to the demons though. Neera, Vel Spren, and I were walking towards Talkra.

I could see the demon, of course. It stood nearly twenty men tall. Six arms danced with blades as long as ten men. Two arms held an impossibly long spear. Its lower body resembled a snake. The upper body resembled a beautiful, if cruel woman.

Neera said, "I have a plan. If you can help me defeat this one, I can consume her. That will give me power to defeat the other. We can win. As you have said, we can heal this wrong."

I shook my head, "No, Neera. You would become a far greater wrong. Braden did not send us here to consume demons. There is something else."

As I spoke, the first sword slammed down at me. It impacted against my divine barrier with a shockwave that spawned tornados around us. I pointed forward. "See? Our enemy helps mask our approach." Vel Spren smiled and began to run towards Talkra.

Neera did not. She stayed behind and summoned images of us. She parried the demon's next sword strike with her own sword while she resumed her Embros shape to counter-attack. It would have seemed brave, except that Neera coveted the demon's power. You see, the slaads gain power by consuming knowledge. To consume such a powerful demon would no doubt allow her to ascend to what she called an 'anthracos.' I'm often very glad she did not succeed.

Demons are fueled by conflict and an Embros battling the demon drew the second demon to their battle. I felt Set's Dream wash out over Neera's battle and thanked Braden we could not see whatever reality changes Neera made. It would no doubt be something terrible, to a demon. I can only imagine its effect on a mortal mind. For our part, Vel and I entered Talkra unchallenged and there, we found Galthrest.

He was struggling to cast a spell. He was tortured, bent, and starving to death. At my touch, he healed. Imagine my hand as if it were Galthrest's. Even after all this time, my hands are those of a warrior. His hands were slender and delicate, like a dancer's. Yet, they had been tortured. He was mumbling to himself something about Lady Magic and not needing his hands. They were so swollen, and infected. When they healed, they practically shed like a snake's skin.

I will never forget the look of cautious hope in his face. He tried to say something and flinched. I helped him open his mouth and saw what the demons had done to his mouth. His tongue! They had torn it out and spiked it with bones from demons. His mouth festered with maggots. I wept to see it. I can put myself back in that place and weep still. I wish his hands and mouth were the only broken parts of him. It took nearly eight healings to restore him, and alas, the madness of despair outside of Time could not be cured.

He grabbed me and exclaimed, "Are you real? You must be. Are you a demon trick, to heal me and then break me again? No, no. You feel holy, and they are vile. I do not wish to ask it, you may be an angel after all, but these heads... the demons love their pain. Prove to me, please, if you are a servant of Creation..."

And, I finally had a chance to study the heads. The demons had bound Galthrest in the center of a large courtyard in front of the Granary, Talkra's capitol building. It was burning and had been shattered. The Great Library of Talkra had long ago burned, but it smoldered still. The courtyard was ringed in a perfect circle, and circles within circles, of severed heads on pikes. The heads lived still.

Comprehending their existence, I realized and Galthrest dropped to his knees at my feet and begged. "If you are an angel, please free them! They were captured trying to save me! I don't know where their bodies are or how the demons keep them alive in pain..."

"Galthrest, I am not an angel, but I do serve the god Braden who is part of Heaven. Even without your request, I will end this atrocity. Release." At my word's, the heads fell quiet and their souls fled to heaven.

Galthrest was sobbing. I have never seen or heard of an archmage crying. He had been humbled. He kept saying over and over again, "If you are an angel, end me too, release me too. Please, Lady Magic, do not let this be another demon trick, dare I? Might I? If you are an angel... Lady Magic..."

I touched his head and blessed him. "I am not a demon. Look, Galthrest, you can see them fighting west of us. Merakor is fallen but it's people are not lost. I lead a band of survivors in an exodus eastwards. I was led to you. I believe you can help them. It is your mission."

"No no no… no more. Please, tell this Braden I am done. I cannot face the Drow again. I cannot." He looked at the demons and began to tremble. I blessed him again and he calmed a bit.

"Archmage, you are all that is left of what you call Lady Magic. You alone were chosen by Braden for this great chore. I do not know what it is, but I bless you that you will know it. Only when you have fulfilled this, will your life be your own again." I wanted to tell him his madness would ease and he would be free. But, Braden cautioned me. Heaven designed us so that our creation would give us both light and dark. Galthrest alone could make the choice to help us, or not.

I waited. Galthrest told me that I was just a dream. He said, "I have spent years now making ready to end myself, to use my life to power my magic to slice the demons in half with a gate of such massive size I would wield it like a sword. Then, you touched me. I have never felt anything like it. It nourished me, restored me. I felt the curses leave and health take root in my old bones. You saved me, though I guess your presence here, now, suggests I am not yet healed."

"You must come with us," I said to him. He nodded. And, just like that, we walked out of Talkra.

After we returned Galthrest to our camp, I went back for Neera. She was wounded and had dealt wounds to the demons. That she still fought impressed me. I healed and blessed her and then entered the combat as her support. Not as a fighter mind you, but to observe and to be ready. I could not believe that Braden would not wish to heal the malign disease that was these demons. But, like Neera, Braden works in strange ways.

I see you laugh to imagine me, and my god, allied with an Embros against demons. It is ironic, I know… and quite Tanian to use a popular parlance these days. But, in that battle, the longer I watched, the more convinced I became that even these had a role to play as well. Night turned back to day and I noticed a cloud of dust on the southern horizon. The dust cloud was easy to know – it was an army.

I began walking towards it. Neera followed, fighting to protect my back as our enemies pressed forward.

Apparently, our exodus had drawn attention. For, while none could endure Braden, our passage lit the land alight with health. We had been followed from the southern Triopolis to Talkra. An army had been sent to intercept us. I saw banners I did not recognize, but Neera knew them.

Perhaps trusting me to heal her, Neera increased the ferocity of her attacks and focused on just one of the demons. She at last killed it and the other retreated a distance. We hoped the demon would leave the world. Instead, it began opening gates to bring in more of demons.

Neera laughed. "I would consume this one and – empowered – destroy the other, but with an army coming and your resistance to the idea… I choose to not." ***

I nodded. "You continue to make wise choices, Neeralyx."

"Those banners are the Imperial Drow House of Ka'ix, the emperor and son of their dark gods, Lolth and Graz'zt. Ka'ix is a god. We should leave." She flexed her hands. "Or… I could consume and ascend, and fight more strongly. You say wisdom is remaining weak?"

I said, "No, I said you are making wise choices. You are not a trustworthy judge of weak and strong, Neera. Look at the things you have done since joining us. The former you would consider these things strong, maybe even Anthracos strong. Maybe you have another path besides Anthracos?" My words reached Neera; they sometimes did.

"I defeated a type nine. No Embros, allied or not, has done such a thing in single combat. That I faced two, perhaps you are right, Nameless."

She had these moments of almost-conversion and I admit it, I loved Neera for those moments. Also, watching the banners and pondering with Braden the knowledge of the Drow Imperial Army, I at last knew what we had to do.

"I know now what they are to do, Neera!" I felt energy and excitement even as Braden filled my mind with trials to come. "We must buy our people time to continue eastwards, to Gateway. They must go to Gateway with all due haste. No rest. They must run. The archmage will open a gate. There is a god ready to receive them to safety." Inspiration comes at the strangest times. I prayed to Braden to carry my words to Vel Spren and Galthrest. By what happened next, I know they received my words.

Neera licked her lips. "Safety? What is safe from the Drow?"

"I do not know, Neera. We must trust in the gods. Galthrest is why we came this far. We must delay this army for them to escape. This exodus is all that remains of Merakor. This story cannot end here. Merakor and its lessons must survive to inform future generations."

* * *

The army stopped a thousand paces from me. I walked forward as siege weapons and wizards prepared to send death my way. Neera swiped her sword side to side and walked boldly at my side. I realize what a strange pair we were!

When their weapons and spells fired, it was if the horizon jumped into the sky. Everything landed around us. Spells that would drop a platoon detonated away from us or in mid-air. Nothing could touch us because Braden had a mission for me.

I pointed to the emperor and continued to advance. They fired on us seven times before they sent half-spider half-paladin Drow to attack. Why did we not slay both type nine demons? This must be why. Similar to how Neera jealously guarded me, the surviving type nine must have decided she wanted me for herself, or maybe that's a delusion of grandeur. More likely, the demon wanted a richer bounty and so attacked the Drow. The demon bowled into Ka'ix's army, as did the summoned demons swarming through the gates.

I found myself in the Longmel battle again. I felt Kargoth's puppet strings attempting to reattach. I still feel them sometimes, even now. But, I was too slippery for Kargoth and paid them no mind. Neera laughed and pointed her sword at the Drow emperor. In their strange tongue, she called out a challenge. It must have been insulting because the emperor sprang forward on his nightmare steed as did all of their female priestesses. The ground between us erupted in spider sacs that belched venomous spiders into the air. Webs and wind swept the spiders towards us.

Like the attacks before, the spiders could not find us. Behind the emperor stood what must have been a personal guard. I barely saw the emperor. You see, in his personal guard, I saw two Drow and Braden whispered to me about them. The emperor attacked me and Neera parried. They were yelling at each other, something about violating a contract with Neeral'oth.

Two of personal guard gleamed in my vision. Only these two were afire with other ways of thinking. For the rest of the Drow, I could see Lolth's influence in them all and knew their fate: centuries of civil war would follow Merakor's exodus. The Drow would all die, or suffer and die, or yearn for death. Being drunk on chaos, they would not recognize it as suffering. The Drow would never be the same. In these two alone I saw something else: regret.

Like me before my conversion to Braden, they regretted where they were. I had to reach them.

I have learned that I am not invulnerable. Powerful magic, divine intervention, the gods, and those who really want to can hurt me. And, I do feel pain. I can die. If I die, I imagine that is it. My life will be weighed against my sins and that will be that. I welcome judgement and accept my eternal consequences as they are. My sins are written in the scars on my body and the souls I took know who I am.

Back then, though, I did not realize I could die. I should have approached these two more nimbly and with more caution. Swords and spiders and spells began to bite into me, and for the first time in years, I felt pain. Braden, I realize now, expects my intelligent service and faith. He cannot see to every aspect of my well-being.

I remember dodging aside from a sword strike that would have decapitated me. Behind me, Neera now dueled the Drow emperor. I'm told it was epic, exactly the kind of legendary thing you might expect of an Embros versus an unascended god.

I had my own battle to fight and I stood within a ring of Drow steel and malice. Swords, poisoned blades, and magical spells came at me faster than I could imagine. Though I cannot remember my name, I remembered being a War Master. I remembered Kargoth's training. Their attacks mostly missed and then my hands closed on the lapel of one of the two Drow I sought. I grappled him to the ground and used his body and armor as my shield as I prayed. "Though I do not know you, I bless you with this gift: insight. This war will end, but Lolth's tyranny of your people will never end unless you find a way to end it."

As he was pulled away from me, he whispered his name: Malyx Do'Allaris. The other was named Invri Vel.

I wish I could say that I fought off the army. The truth is that they captured me. Neera was forced to retreat and probably would have died had Vel Spren and the Three Druids not saved her. The Drow took me and let the others go. They believed that without me the exodus would end.

For days, they tried to kill me and grew bolder and bolder in their experiments against me. Like the slaad stabbing me with its sword, they studied and sought ways to inflict pain, to bypass Braden's protection. I felt some of it. Others I did not. My tormentors felt all of it. Each day that passed was more time for the survivors to attain Gateway, for Galthrest to find his mission.

For days, Malyx and Invri would bring me water and urge me to tell Ka'ix what he wished to know: how had I evaded the Drow with so many for so long. Under their breath, they would ask about life and living, and I would answer for them what it means to truly choose, to truly live.

You see, most confuse the ability to choose with the ability to choose good or evil. It is not the same thing. While most societies regard theft as evil, a starving child taking bread in the midst of hunger is not a choice the child gets to make. Their hunger overrides their ability to make a moral choice. To judge such an act as evil in hindsight is, in itself, evil.

I told them both, "Lolth has so clouded the Drow thinking that you think you are waging a war of vengeance. Here is your folly: Lolth does not care which race of Elves is mightiest or rightest. She cares only for the chaos that war brings. After this war," I told them, "and it will end – you will turn on each other because that is what your chosen goddess craves. You lost your ability to morally choose and determine your own lives when you chose to serve an abyssal goddess."

I suggest they look at their tools of war: manipulation, brother against brother, murder, and indiscriminate use of demons. I said, "If these are your tools of vengeance, you must logically conclude that these same tools will be used by your priesthood against you. The havoc it brought Merakor is a foreshadow of what awaits your entire people." I pointed it out; was that what they wanted for the Drow? We know from the Lord Daryx, the Malyx I speak of now, that this is exactly what happened. I sometimes wish Braden had compelled me to prophesy of this to the Drow army rather than just these two fighters.

They wanted to know what they could do. I told them the truth: do something different that is not what the priestesses tell you to do. I had to explain this many different ways before they began to see and understand. "Though there may only be a few sides in a war, when Merakor is fallen, it really becomes one side with many agendas. Are you serving a god or an agenda? You can bet that Lolth's agenda is simple: the chaos of war. That's it. There is nothing else. This is the abyss. If you do not believe me, study the spiders. See how they weave webs and look at where action and interest occur. All is peaceful until a strand is broken or prey is caught. That is all there is to Lolth."

Eventually, an illness began to grow in the Drow camp. Those who sought to torture me, those who wounded me became ill. Healing, and healing magic, was denied them. Like Neeralyx's broken fangs, they could not recover.

Braden is the god of healing. By offending me, they offend the dominion of healing and so Braden stripped them from the succor of his dominion. I repeatedly explained this to them after my capture.

In a panic, they began coming to me for healing and I would not. They tried to torture me, as Lolth is wont to do… and when they began to die it confirmed the rumors of what they called the 'Braden Curse.' I know my god does not like having the word 'curse' ascribed to his name, but for the Drow, I was – I am personally just fine with it.

Ka'ix came to me eventually. He offered me whatever I wanted to revoke the curse. I smiled and said, "Kill me, emperor. My god does not wish to aid your dark purpose."

He said, "If I kill you, I know I will die. No, you will remove this curse or we will destroy those who follow you."

Mentally, I had been tracking the exodus and Braden assured me that they were almost to safety. They needed two more days at least. I met the emperor's eyes and I said, "If you will repent of this war, I will pray to Braden and ask that this curse be removed."

I remember his eyes narrowing and he repeated the ancient Merakoran word I had used: *repentance*. "You mean this in the sense of total restitution and forsaking this, all of this?" He laughed. His laughter hurt. Remembering his laughter now makes my head hurt. It was not altogether the laughter of any elf I have ever met.

He walked away and monsters were summoned to torture me. They brought in slaves to lash at me with bone-spiked flails. I confess to screaming until I was hoarse. With each flaying of my skin, I counted another moment for the exodus. Braden felt my pain, and the curse extended to the mages and those ordering or compelling others to hurt me. By midnight, no one would touch me. You see, it was not just healing magic that was denied. Magics that restored youth or compensated for old wounds or disabilities came undone too. Perhaps, and for the first time since the Race Wars, the Drow were forced to see some of their own in an unvarnished state.

When dawn rose the next morning, Vel Spren attacked the Drow host. It was the last great stand of Merakor against the Drow. She had given herself to the All Father... for me. I did not recognize her at first because she fell on the Drow like a silver comet. Her fire divided their army in half. My exodus had found remnants of other Merakoran armies gathered at Gateway. Their charge followed her fire.

At her attack, my bonds fell away and my two students, Malyx and Invri, took me away from the war host in disguise. I blessed them both with an unknowable journey that could save their people, if they would but find another way.

Silvespren, the silver dragon, was beautiful. Her grace and light made my heart sing. Vel Spren loved dragons and now she was one. I hurried north to Gateway and that was when I saw her fall. I stood on the hill overlooking Talkra to my left. The southern plains, once so green with corn and other crops, now presented a battle that my old self would have rejoiced to see. Kargoth wanted me to see the ugliness of the Drow and take revenge, but I was as captivated by Silvespren as I was when I first met her, and my sword spared both our lives.

She did not attack alone. A thousand fighters from our journey joined. Neera rode on her back. I saw them point to me as they wheeled before the Drow. Then, the Embros fell from Silvespren's back into the Drow hordes like a bomb. I was so proud of them both, but my heart ached to see Silvespren's mounting wounds and fatigue. When she at last fell to the ground and did not rise up again, I wept, and I ran with all my might for Gateway.

I found the exodus organized into columns twenty people across. Galthrest cast a mighty spell with every mage and every magic item possessed by the group laid out before the columns. The rows stretched across Gateway and throughout its wide boulevards. The Three Sisters greeted me and gave me a letter from Vel Spren. I have held this for a very long time. I'm going to read it to you now. At last, Braden tells me it is time. You see, the world is changing. I have ached to read this letter. I can barely breathe. I am excited but also terrified to do this in front of you all.

> *Nameless Master, I write to you with both joy and sorrow in my heart. I have given myself to the All Father and must buy the exodus time. Like you, I am willing to sacrifice all that I am for the exodus to save Merakor, the land I love. I regret I did not get to tell you my true feelings. I love you. I love you so deeply I cannot imagine a world where we are not together. Fate whispers to me that I will see you in Creation's light one day. Our love will be my weapon. My hope of your love, my armor. Our journey to Gateway with our tens of thousands will be the tale I sing to the Heavens. I will find this Braden God and tell him of your deeds.*

> *Beloved, your name is Renault cul Longmel. You are, were, the king of the Longmels. You are a hero who defeated a Blind Dragon and did many other feats of renown. Word reached Lyrion that you had sided with the Drow. That is why your family died. Neeralyx, one of his spawn, delivered this rumor to Lyrion. Another of his spawn led the knights that murdered your family. Neera tells me that the Drow had*

another name for you: Master of War. They whispered your name like a dark prayer. That is who you were.

I tell you this that you may know for what purpose you seek redemption. I believe in your redemption. I will hold a place for you in my heart, in Heaven, in the sun of Creation, for you always.

I have another favor to ask of you. Should you endure, and should any of my family endure, I would that you give them this note. Tell my brother Pajor that I love and miss him. I forgive him for sending me away from Kinpeace; it saved my life. I forgive Mother and Father for banishing my house; it saved us all. I think fondly of our family and choose to remember our lofty banners flying atop Havkor's towers. I choose to remember you giving me horseyback rides in the Sylvan Forests. If any of you survive, please know that I chose the All Father and am ascended as a silver dragon. I am of the House of Vel. I choose Heaven. My heart is your heart, and you are all in my heart forever.

With all my love,
Vel Spren

* * *

I look up while fingering the silver dragon scale around my neck and say, "I do not remember the name of Renault. I do remember massacring all of the Longmels, thinking I was serving Merakor and Lyrion. I do not remember being a Master of War, but I remember having mastered warfare."

I pull on the silver dragon scale and it splits into two scales pressed together. One is inscribed to me with Vel Spren's love. The other is inscribed to Vel Pajor. "Vel Spren wishes that I give this to you. The god of necromancy is fallen. Orcus is dead. The world is changing. I do not remember being who I was, but I remember Vel Spren's love. It is time, great king of Morilon, to repent of the regret poisoning your life. It is time that you know this: your sister lived and chose each step of her life. She died a hero. She loves you. I know this as surely as I am standing her giving you this last token of her life."

I take Vel Pajor's hand. Around us, his spellbound guard shakes out of their reverie. They do not like anyone touching Vel. I press the dragon scale into his hand. "Read the inscription."

He does not want to. Gray elves are especially stubborn. I pull his hand and the scale up to his face. "Do not make me call on Braden to heal your sight. This is from your sister!"

Vel opens his eyes and reads what is written there. Tears begin to flow and the great king of Morilon flees my presence. The guards itch to follow but I bid them stay, and they do.

"Sometimes, the hurt we inflict on ourselves is a greater sin than the regrets rooting at the base of that hurt. Let your king mourn his sister." I look around Morilon. It is beautiful here, exactly like Vel Spren described the elven gardens in the Triopolis to me.

"If possible, she told me of a song beloved by Vel Pajor. Let it play and let silver lights fill the world tree of Morilon. I prayed to have brought this to your people and king sooner, but Braden did not allow it. With the Necromancer fallen, the world changes. I rejoiced when the winds brought me here. Bring me your sick as I leave, and let Morilon be blessed."

The guard nods and I turn to leave. The wind is blowing and Morilon was just a stop in my eternal atonement. Outside, I hear Vel Pajor weeping.

I do not remember this Renault. I do not know my name.

ERIC K. BARNUM

CREATION
THE TEMPLE OF THE GOLDEN SERPENT

The Temple of the Golden Serpent: Pel Paijan

Lord Daryx,

I hope this message finds you hale and prosperous. As requested, here is a full and detailed copy of the testimony of Jerranic, faithful battle priest of the Literalist Order of Pha Rann. You should have already received Jerranic's summarized report to King Andrew upon his return from the Western Lands, as recorded by duly trained and sworn Temple scribes. I jotted a few notes in the margins where I thought you might need background information.

Please accept all the usual disclaimers about this being an eyewitness account and therefore subject to the veracity and understanding of the eyewitness, but Jerranic is not a fool nor is he a man given to exaggeration. After the summarized interview, His Highness dismissed Jerranic without saying much, and guessing the royal mind is far above my pay grade, so I cannot say how seriously he took this report. For what it's worth, however, the Literalist High Mage Radcliffe was in attendance when Jerranic gave this account, and I'm told the old man's face went as white as his beard. Jerranic gave a much more in-depth assessment afterwards to the Literalist Temple, which is contained herein.

Like Morbatten, the death of a high priest is a serious matter. Please understand that an inquest has already happened and Jerranic's party is found completely blameless of High Priest Olimen's death along with Lovik, an up and coming healer. Should you have any questions in this matter, I can send you the inquest hearings. No atonement rites were sanctioned.

This record is entrusted to Morbatten through the Queen's Way and the Kingdom of Harkenwood, friend of the Literalist Order… and so on and so forth, we both know the official wording… look Daryx, I'm not going to even pretend to ask you not to show this to Dar Ana and the Dread Lords, but if you and I are friends at all, burn these papers soon. The Temples are proceeding with their own investigation into the drugs brought back by this quest. I've enclosed a small sample of each. As is our right in the Queen's Way, I ask that any findings by Morbatten are shared back to me.

May the Sun Shine Always,
King of Harkenwood, Alaur unt Scott in the Morbatten Year of 1809 DAR

The Unabridged Testimony of Jerranic

In my own words, freely and candidly? As you wish, my lord. But, may I ask, do you wish full details or just the higher-level points as did the High King? Very well, full details. I will start with Lovik, a healer in our Order.

Lovik was almost dead when they brought him to the ship. Pa Haram's guards had found him and brought him to us, recognizing him as a foreigner. Staggering around the docks. Pale, shaking, sweating, could barely breathe or speak. We brought him back to the ship and Olimen and I spent five days trying to figure out what the blazes was wrong with him and how we could fix it.

Well, I say "we," but he's the high priest and he was stumped, so what good was I going to be? I spent much of those five days reading my Dialectics and keeping Olimen's daughter, Sidney, out of his hair as best I could. She's a sweet kid, I'm sure she'll make a great healer one day, but daughter of the high priest or not, she's only six and she was ready to climb the walls, especially after things got tense with the minotaurs and Olimen confined her to our rooms on the world galleon. Though the minotaurs were worried about disease, Olimen knew Lovik's illness was not contagious. I don't know how he knew, though we both assumed it a disease.

Anyway, poor Lovik. Speaking of kids, I'm pretty sure Lovik was only nineteen or twenty, but he was an up and comer. He had a future in the Order. I think that trip was probably his first major assignment, and he'd only been out for a week; he was one of the advance scouts we sent inland. His initial symptoms only got worse. He sweated constantly and could barely talk or swallow. He was having increasing trouble breathing, and between that and the pain, he never slept for more than a few minutes.

But the worst was the fits. He came in shaking, but by the end of the first day shaking became spasms, then spasms became full blown seizures. You could see the seizures coming. His... ribcage, his entire torso, would start to catch and heave like tremors before an earthquake. Then, when the seizure came on, his whole body would clench like I've never seen a human body do. You would have been able to tell it hurt like hell even if he weren't screaming the whole time, which he was.

Oh, the screaming. Pha Rann bless me, it was unbearable. When there were any words to it, they were *help me* or *kill me* or *make it stop*. Occasionally you'd catch a few words of one of our prayers. But mostly it was just wordless mewling and croaking, like... a dog run over by an oxcart or something. It was enough to make the hairs on your arms stand up, and it just went on and on and on. And he'd puke. Not always, but some of the time a mouthful of something dark, clotted, and rank would come out of him. Which was alarming, because he hadn't had anything to eat in days.

Once a seizure started, it only ended when it ended, sometimes long after he had stopped breathing and we feared he would die. When he at last released, you'd have a few hours of relative peace before the next one. Pha Rann forgive me, but by the third day I wanted to smother him just to give him some peace! It wouldn't have taken much. I even started to think of it as an act of kindness. Kindness to him, though, or just to me? I would have done almost anything not to have to sit and wait for the next seizure, powerless to...

I'm sorry. Please forgive me. I guess you can see how I ended up a battle priest. I don't know how the healers do it. Even Sidney, Pha Rann bless her, showed me for a weakling those days. She stood right there with her clean little wash rag, brave little smile, ready to help.

Between fits, Lovik would become more or less lucid, though in apparent pain. Those were the only times he was any kind of help in his own diagnosis, so Olimen would try and talk to him as much as possible before he lapsed back into moaning and groaning.

It was during one such lucid moment on the fifth day, I think after his second big seizure that day, that Lovik gave us our breakthrough. He rolled and twisted away from us on the bed, which he had done plenty of times before, but this time he screamed something about the sun. I want to say it was something like "Get it away! Get it away! The sun, it burns!" Now keep in mind that the only light in that cabin was a single candle in one of the sconces. It was barely enough to read by. We knew perfectly well by that point that Lovik was very light sensitive, but something about those words startled me. I guess it startled Olimen too, because he stopped in the middle of whatever he had been meditating about and looked straight at me.

It wasn't just that Lovik had mistaken a candle for the sun; delirium could explain that, and Lovik had been serving up fever dream nonsense to us for five days by then. *It was that he thought the sun was something to panic over.* As you know, my lord, it takes quite a lot to make one of ours despise the sun.

My mind was reeling. My immediate thought was that we had somehow missed the early signs of vampirism or some other form of necromantic disease. I probably would have said so except that in that moment I realized Sidney had come back into the room and was standing at my elbow. Pha Rann keep me, am I ever so glad of that interruption. Not just because I would have been wrong. I mean, the truth ended up being so monstrous and so strange that none of us could have guessed it from the start. But Olimen is the high priest, you know? To suggest that we had been sitting by a vampire for five days and missed all the signs would really be saying that *he* missed all the signs.

Seeing Sidney standing by me, Olimen took his open prayer book and stood it on the table so that it blocked the candle's direct light from reaching Lovik. That seemed to calm him down some, though he was still groaning and wheezing. Olimen looked at Sidney, then at me, and his eyes locked on mine for a long few seconds. I'm no mind reader, and Olimen isn't usually the most demonstrative fellow, but I understood the look perfectly. He was saying *my daughter is very sharp, but she's just a small child. Be very careful of what you say and how you say it.*

As if to make his point for him, Sidney tugged my sleeve and said, "What happened? Do you know what's wrong with Lovik now?"

I opened my mouth, not even sure of what I was going to say, but Sidney wasn't done yet. She patted my cheek and said, "Bless him! Heal him! Pha Rann cures what's wrong with you." The last part, she did in that sing-song voice, like the little rhymes we teach to toddlers, and was patting my cheek in time with the song. I don't know why – maybe shock over what we had just learned, maybe just the simple purity of her faith – but I started to get tears in my eyes. I might have lost it entirely and started weeping if Olimen hadn't interrupted.

"Battle Priest Jerranic, in your studied opinion, what is wrong with Brother Lovik?" His voice was businesslike and his phrasing more formal than he usually used with me, and it snapped me back instantly. As I took a deep breath, I realized he had done that intentionally. Bless him.

I summarized what we already knew: five days of worsening symptoms, some of which shifted and changed, but the constants were sensory aggravation, perspiration, and difficulty breathing.

He said, "And in light of recent developments, what is your diagnosis and prognosis?" Still in that formal tone as if I were an acolyte rather than a battle priest. In the moment I was almost offended, but… by talking to me like a student, he helped me re-examine what we already knew in the new light of what we had just learned. I get it now. Blazes, he's brilliant. Make that one more time I'm grateful I kept my mouth shut in front of the high priest.

Prognosis was easy. I said that if things went on as they were, either lack of sleep or dehydration would take him, and soon. He might be past the threshold already. Lovik's outburst didn't change any of that. And I didn't need to point out that things weren't just going on; they were getting worse.

As far as diagnosis went, I pointed out that the symptoms resembled a few poisons, but more than anything they resembled drug withdrawal. This was my almost-epiphany. Withdrawal didn't make sense though, because it should get better with the passage of time, not worse. And neither condition of poison or addiction would explain the way we'd seen his spirit flagging; the simple orison to detect good or evil showed a flickering aura around Lovik, not the steady glow you'd normally expect. Spiritual poison? Spiritual drug withdrawal? It made no sense. Finally I said that if I didn't know any better, I might guess that Lovik had contracted *Dolums Somnum*, which is endemic to the Western Lands. I told Sidney what *Dolums Somnum* meant. Or tried to, anyway.

"Painful sleep," she said. "I *know* that." She gave me a look that, if she were twelve instead of six, would probably have included an eye roll. Out of the corner of my eye, I saw Olimen smiling. I smiled too. Like I said, smart kid. Can't be mad at her.

We realized that Lovik had stopped groaning. He had turned back to face us and was struggling to half-sit, straining towards us. His eyes were mostly clear. Olimen turned and eased Lovik back down onto it. He had gotten good at managing Lovik during those brief respites, all soft tones and reassurance, while trying to get as much information out of him as possible. Olimen launched right away into the questions we had agreed to ask during his next lucid moment – we had a list.

"I'd take your hand in fellowship," Olimen said, "but I'm concerned it will hurt you, Lovik. Tell me, when you were with the Paijans, did you follow our Temple's diet regimen strictly?" As soon as Lovik started to shake his head, Olimen said, "Yes, of course you did. Can you think of anything you might have done, or might have encountered, to expose yourself to disease?"

Lovik shook his head again, more vigorously. The movement made him groan and he started groping around for his vomit bucket. But, thankfully it did not start another fit and Lovik gave up and collapsed back onto the bed without throwing up.

"Don't answer," Olimen said. "Of course you did not, would not. I know Jerranic and the others have asked you a hundred times, but please think about your travels again. Pray to Pha Rann for guidance and find what may be missing from your recollection."

To my surprise, Lovik began to pray. Barely recognizable through his parched throat and bleeding lips, but it was the *Lux Reperio* prayer, the Light of Finding. Without looking back at me, Olimen held out his hand and I gave him his ledger, the one where he had been keeping his questions and answers. In one section Olimen had running notes about Lovik's symptoms. Olimen skipped that section and went to the record of all the things that Lovik had said – the ones that made sense, anyway. I had been helping Olimen try and reconstruct the timeline of Lovik's week away from the boat out of these fragments, without much success.

Olimen started flipping through the pages, almost at random. His lips were moving. I don't know which prayer, or even if it was a prayer at all. Augury perhaps? After a few moments, Olimen stopped with his finger on a page, and it looked like an early page to me. He looked up from the page into Lovik's eyes. They were feverish, sunken, and exhausted, but clear, for a few more minutes at least.

"Tell me about what you called the Golden Temple." As soon as Olimen started talking, my head popped up. His voice wasn't any louder, but it contained a note of command that was in complete contrast to the soothing tones he'd been using.

The Golden Temple? I remembered the reference, but Lovik had said it early on and I hadn't been present for that one. It had come out in the midst of a bunch of nonsense, so we'd collectively decided to dismiss it as delirium, or at least put it aside. As you know, I described the Golden Temple in some detail for the High King so we can skip that part. Paladin Tomas also provided detailed descriptions.

Lovik had snapped to attention at the change in Olimen's voice as well. He was trying to respond, but had trouble catching his breath. Olimen reached out, grabbed Lovik's hand, and used one of the healing prayers. Then he said, "May that strengthen you so that we may learn how to truly heal you."
Lovik drew a deep breath – the first real breath I'd heard him take in days – and his face got a little color back. I was shocked; I mean, of course I knew that Olimen's powers exceeded my own, but I hadn't been able to achieve anything remotely close to what he managed with that short

prayer. As a battle priest, I pride myself on exceedingly fast prayer evocations.

I knew that when the gift expired – and I was curious to know how much longer his prayer would last than mine had – the symptoms would come back many times worse. Olimen knew it too, of course. Worst of all, I'm sure Lovik knew it. The exaggerated return of symptoms was the reason we had stopped trying to heal him directly.

Lovik put his other hand on top of Olimen's, clasping Olimen's hand in both of his. When he spoke, it was clearer than it had been since his return. Still pained, and halting, but so much better than before. He said, "A young family took their newborn to the Golden Temple. It's a ritual they all do. They invited me. I had been hearing about this Temple from others." Lovik took another deep breath. "A one-day trip with a new infant. She would have died without Pha Rann healing them, or Lovik's using his medical training to assist. The baby too."

Olimen patted Lovik's hand with his free hand. "You did the right thing. But your time is short with us, Lovik. Please, the Golden Temple. What else?"

"Was beautiful! The Temple of Sun in ancient Lyrion could not have shined brighter. The Great Temple in Sora… a hedge witch shrine by comparison." Lovik blinked a few times, a quick flutter of eyelids. He looked at me for a second before turning his attention back to Olimen. "Glorious. Made me want to sing to Pha Rann. Angels! Gold, silver light everywhere. A testament to Heaven. But also not… they do not know what it truly is. The people do not know." Lovik closed his eyes and seemed to deflate. "I never figured it out. Something dark is there wearing a beautiful face."

Olimen nodded and urged Lovik to continue. I shared his impatience. It had been several minutes, and I could tell Olimen didn't know any better than I did how long this would last. My gut feeling was that this might be the last chance we had to learn anything new from Lovik. He was uncommonly focused right now, though his pallor was worsening with each second.

I feel as if I should feel bad about watching a man die and feeling impatient to pump him for information, but I did not then and still do not reflecting on it now. I think we all knew Lovik was done for, but could help those of us left alive. Blazes, but I would wager Lovik knew his time had come too. If it had been me on the bed, I know I would have felt the same, compassion be damned.

"I tried to sing to Pha Rann," Lovik said. "Temple had thin spires lifting up. To Heaven. Angels carved on the front with… offerings. Food, healing. Love. But also humans offering these treasures to a golden serpent. Thought it was their rep… representation of the All Father, or even Pha Rann."

Olimen looked over his shoulder at me and asked, "Perhaps Sidney could go fetch Tomas and Vindi? I'd like them here for consultation." I took him saying it to me rather than her directly as a hint: Olimen wanted her gone for a while. My stomach started to knot. I looked at Sidney; she was standing with that very serious face she gets sometimes. Not scared – I've still never seen the kid cry – just very intent. Her medical bandages and linens were on the floor between her feet. She hadn't even noticed that she'd dropped it.

I tore a corner of paper from my own notebook and wrote a quick note to the paladin Tomas: COME TO LOVIK'S CABIN. TELL SIDNEY TO STAY THERE WITH VINDI. –J.

I folded the paper and sent Sidney down the corridor to deliver it. A second after she ran out the door, the whole ship lurched, causing the door to slam shut behind her. It was the galleon running aground in the low tide, our twice daily reminder of where we were.

Lovik pulled his hands free of Olimen's and tried again to sit up. This time, Olimen didn't stop him, just pushed his pillows around to kind of support him in a half-sitting position. I saw new sweat beginning to bead on Lovik's brow. It had to be more than five minutes since Olimen's prayer by that time, but I was losing track. My most fervent prayers had only ever brought Lovik half a minute of peace.

Yes, my lord. I realize that comparative analysis is a Tanian thing. I probably picked this up while training at their Temple. It's useful. Yes. Okay, I will stop discussing Olimen's power compared to my own. Back to Lovik.

"Inside, air smelled like sugar." Lovik's voice was growing thin again. His breath was getting raspy. "Priest. Had a golden drape... cloth... over face. Took the baby and washed her in a great fountain. Glowing sweet water. I heard the baby giggle. Impossible. A newborn giggling! Thought I was hearing things."

Lovik tried to take another deep breath, but he coughed and lurched forward. He looked at me for a second, and I saw his pupils were dilating. But unevenly – one was big and the other was huge. I didn't have to be a healer to guess that wasn't a good sign; I've brained enough people with my mace over the years, thanks be to Pha Rann. I mentally prepared to assist Olimen in commending Lovik's soul to Heaven.

"The golden serpent. Is not All Father. Not Heaven." And just like that, the lucidity was gone. Lovik arched backwards so hard that his head smacked the wall behind his bed. He was screaming, but without breath. I can't swear to it, but I think I heard his ribs snap. Awful. I just wanted it to be over. But it wasn't yet. Once that first spasm let go, he took a breath and started screaming for real, started clawing at himself. At his arms and chest. He went to claw at his face. Olimen reached out to grab him by the wrists, I was surprised how fast he moved, but it didn't matter. Lovik's whole body went limp and he sank back onto the bed.

He was dead.

My lord, there are no diseases or poisons or venoms or anything that create days-long symptoms like this. This is what perplexed us so badly. With what I know now, we could have taken a different approach but I'm still not confident we could have saved Lovik. My summary of this to the King… Okay. You want me to continue chronologically? Very well.

Olimen slumped beside Lovik's bed. He was leaning against the bed and looking up at me. He looked exhausted. He bowed his head and said, "So passes Lovik, faithful follower of Light, brother-in-arms, servant to Pha Rann's children."

I didn't know what to say. I've seen plenty of people die in my time, had to kill more than a few myself, but I'd never witnessed anything like this. The hardest part of it to come to grips with was how helpless Olimen was, we all were. I'd come up through the ranks thinking of him as the one with all the answers, you know? To see the high priest sitting there on the floor, exhausted, defeated, was just…yeah. I mean, not only did Lovik die, we still hadn't even figured out exactly what was happening! To see Olimen in that position was almost the most surreal part of the whole experience.

But please, my Lord, don't think I'm saying this as criticism, or saying I thought any less of him. I realized that Olimen was just another man, and that maybe all the things he had always made to look so easy were actually hard. He *didn't* know everything. He *did* fail sometimes. His faith *was* shaken, was shakable. If anything, I admired him more in that moment than ever before.

I asked Olimen how this was possible. We had tried everything, I told him. I didn't expect an answer. It sounds stupid when I say it now, but I think I was just trying to tell him in a roundabout way not to blame himself. He did answer, though.

"I must go to this Golden Temple," Olimen said. "We cannot revive Lovik; he will simply die again. We will not make him relive that torment for the sake of interrogation. Please ask our Tauran hosts when they will be leaving. I would like to extend our stay here another week."

And just like that, I was irritated at Olimen again. He knew very well when our ship was scheduled to depart, and he knew perfectly well what he was asking me to do. He was already standing up as he spoke, smoothing out his robes. Maybe after showing vulnerability, he wanted to put me back at arm's length right away?

I told him that I would do as he asked, but that the Taurans weren't going to like it. In that moment, it occurred to me that I was also about to tell the minotaurs that Lovik had died. That was a chilling thought. They're a superstitious lot, as I'm sure you know, my Lord. They hate disease, they especially hate mysterious disease, and above all they hate and fear deaths aboard ship. Do not even get me started on how little they regard the people of Pel Paijan! Lovik was now a perfect combination of everything our crew detested. I had a sudden vision of asking Captain to let us stay there another week and him responding, "Stay as long as you like!" He'd probably say this while throwing us off the ship. I heard footsteps coming up the corridor. Too loud for Sidney, too quiet for minotaurs, so probably Tomas and

Vindi. Olimen heard it too. He looked towards the door while he shrugged the last tangle out of his mantle.

"We will deal with that when we must," he said.

The Taurans wanted exorbitant prices to stay longer in Pa Haram. The minotaur captain, whom I never heard them call anything other than "Captain," stomped a hoof on the foredeck. He pointed across the docks, west toward the horizon. "Hurricanes form and we should ride the wind. Faster than storms made by magic! This delay will cost us not only the week you ask, but two more weeks at least because we let those winds go. The mages and clerics will be exhausted where we could ride the storms for free! You will pay for three weeks' delay!" I considered us fortunate to get off that easily. It bordered on extortion, but what can you do? It is not negotiation when one side has all the power and both sides know it.

Captain also rejected my request to bring Lovik home for proper burial, before I even finished asking. The moment the words *our crew member has died* escaped my lips, he made a couple of finger signs with his hand raised to his right horn, and his boatswain was at our side by the time I finished the sentence. Captain said, in the Common tongue for my benefit, "Send a fire team to the sun priest's chamber."

The crewman ran off as quickly as he'd arrived. Tomas told me later that the "fire team" consisted of their chief mage, the one they called "Storm Master," and two deck hands with brooms. They razed Lovik's chamber with magical fire for almost an hour, down to bare stone. Lovik's body, the bedcovers, all of his belongings, every last thing in the room: ash. Even my copy of the Dialectics, which I'd left under my chair. Luckily I'd left my good copy at home and brought my old student one on the trip. And by Pha Rann's grace, Tomas had the presence of mind to snatch up Olimen's notebooks and slip them into his tabard as they were being hustled out of the room.

After that, the Taurans confined us for real. Captain told me, "You are all in quarantine until we know you are not infected. Until *my* priest says so, Pha Rannic. Baphtomet requires your purity. Of course, you're free to not stay on my ship!"

At the mention of their god's name, I made the expected gesture. I hated doing it, but we were their guests, and I didn't see any good reason to antagonize the minotaurs any further. There's a reason I was sent on that trip rather than a Cuthberic, right? So, I made the damned hand sign and told them we agreed to it. They returned the sign, nodded, and everyone went back to work.

They stuck us in the farthest corner of the cargo hold from the crew decks. Provisions and water were shoved towards us with long poles by minotaurs. Unhappy minotaurs at that: we figured out pretty quickly that feeding the ill-omened Soran clerics was punishment duty.

It was miserable, but I didn't have to deal with it for long. Olimen had decided he needed to see the Golden Temple, whatever it was. And he'd decided Tomas and I would go with him. Vindi stayed with Sidney, and also to make sure the Taurans didn't change their minds and leave. The rest of us packed and prepared to try and retrace Lovik's steps.

Beyond the wind swept coastal bluffs of Pa Haram, the dense jungle covering most of Pel Paijan waited. A mist of clouds hung in the upper foliage that covered all but exposed rock. I had been wishing to go and see it myself. Now, I only felt dread.

* * *

Once we headed inland from the port at Pa Haram, the way to Pel Paijan became jungle quickly. The road itself was well traveled and well kept, but humidity and insects plagued us. Though, I kept noticing how grand the architecture was, especially in the gates leaving Pa Haram. It had been visible at the docks too, but was overshadowed by the Tauran ship. The stones set to make the road seemed worn, but disturbingly, they were cracked and not repaired. We all noticed it.

We had hired a local guide by the name of Jem. He was mostly good for laughing at our discomfort, but he came through with good advice when we needed it most. Eventually. For example, the morning of our first full day on the road, Olimen, Tomas, and I all woke up covered in hard red welts. Our faces, necks, hands, even the bottoms of my feet, because I hate sleeping in my boots, eaten alive by some kind of parasitic insect. As we were touching our faces and gaping at each other, the welts started to itch like mad. Tomas is usually good at the stoic paladin routine, but he started swatting his hands at passing bugs and yelling "Sun burn them all!" I understood how he felt.

We heard a scraping noise and turned to see Jem kneeling a dozen paces away, digging in the ground. He came over to us with a handful of roots, chuckling under his breath. His own skin was clear as day, of course. He handed us each a root. With his pocket knife, he cut his own root in half, and there was a milk-white sap that beaded up on the cut surfaces. It smelled awful, like rotted bird. He dabbed the root against the sides of his neck, the inside of each wrist, and pulled up his pants legs and dabbed some on each ankle. He chuckled some more, I guess because he couldn't believe we didn't know this.

The three of us exchanged looks, then in unison, we tore our roots to pieces and smeared that disgusting slime over every inch of exposed skin and through our hair. That was good for an actual belly laugh from Jem. Thankfully, the smell quickly faded as did the welts.

On the second day, our road began to intersect with other highways. It started to rise in altitude as well. A few hours after lunch that day, we caught our first glimpse of Pel Paijan. Lovik hadn't been lying about the Golden Temple. Even from that distance, you could make out a gleaming dome and tall spires set against a vast cityscape. I was captivated for a few moments by the visible rays and arcs of sunlight shining from that building. I thought it was beautiful, and said so.

Following a few paces behind me, Tomas' reaction was exactly what you'd expect of a Literalist knight. "Jerranic, to find beauty in evil is to compromise your integrity. This *beauty* killed Lovik."

I fought the urge to roll my eyes. Tomas and I didn't see eye to eye on a lot of things, but I was trying not to let things escalate with someone I was going to be sharing a cramped cargo bay with for a month or more. Anyway, I looked over my shoulder and replied that all it was right now was a mystery. A beautiful one.

"An *evil* mystery," Tomas muttered.

I'd had enough. We were in a foreign land and I had just watched my friend die horribly. I was covered in itchy welts and rotting plant slime. I stopped walking and turned towards him. Forgive my saying so, my Lord, but that Order sure loves to recruit the dense and relentless. The way they talk, you'd think there were no sunrise or sunset, no shades of difference between noon and midnight, that Pha Rann simply cuts the sun on and off each day like he was shuttering a lantern.

Olimen chose that moment to interrupt. "Careful, Brother Jerranic," he said. "The Sun shines on all."
Tomas smiled in evident triumph as he passed me.. I felt my face burning. I'm sure I turned red. Instantly, all the resentment I'd been feeling for Tomas became resentment for Olimen – why did only I get a warning?

But, then I understood: *I received the warning because I could handle the warning, and would learn from it.* And just like that, the resentment vaporized. Olimen had snuffed an argument before it turned ugly, and left Tomas and me each feeling like the winner. Far from manipulated, I felt amazed. That's a leader. I'd love to know if that's something Olimen was taught so that he could be a great high priest, or if he became a great high priest because he already knew how.

A few minutes later, Olimen had us stop so he could use a translation prayer on Jem. Jem knew enough of the Tauran language to say a few halting phrases, but not nearly enough for actual conversation.. While Olimen was casting his prayer, Tomas took me aside and said, "The only good for Lovik is to find the evil cause and end it." He put a hand on my shoulder and smiled while he said it. I'm sure even that minimal bit of diplomacy wasn't easy for him, so I smiled back and agreed we needed to end it. For Lovik.

We walked all day through rolling hills, steaming jungle around and below us, never losing sight of those spires. In the early evening, Jem gestured and told us we would reach a village soon. Not too long after that, though, we reached an intersection of our road and what had to be two major highways.

A patrol was waiting there. Not for us, I don't think; just guarding the crossroads. Their shields and helmets all bore the same stylized white hand we had been seeing frequently since we'd arrived in Pel Paijan. We still didn't know exactly what it meant at that point, but Lovik had guessed that it was religious rather than a military or governmental insignia. Half right, I guess. Good instincts on his part, though. As I said before, Lovik had had a promising future.

When we were a few dozen steps from the patrol, Jem motioned us to wait, then stepped forward and started talking to them in a really animated way. Quietly, just on a whim, I chanted the prayer to detect evil intent. I detected nothing but the barest hint of Warp. It was so slight that I wondered if there were something wrong with my prayer. There was no malice in the guards or the situation, though. Standing there, wishing Olimen had extended his translation prayer to me, my eyes were drawn to the ornate armor worn by the guards and their horses. The motif of monsters and heraldic banners showed masterful craftsmanship. But, it was nearly lost by a twisting golden serpent that had been worked on top of whatever the earlier design had been. I wish the serpent was of similar quality. It was not.

The quality of the workmanship between the ornate armor and the newer serpent were striking. The horses' equipment and barding had similar differences. Newer work seemed good, but not as detailed, less refined. My eyes took in the road we had been on. I had interpreted the declining quality of the roadway as a function of distance from Pa Haran in a jungle climate. But, here at what appeared to be a major intersection, the same ill state of repair predominated. I corrected myself while looking at the armor – *neglect*. Somewhere, massive energy and resources were being spent to update the serpent design.

Armor like that, here in Taysor, would be enchanted. We never would entrust such valuable gear to a common patrol *inside* the empire. Maybe during a time of war at a border, or near a monster intrusion, or some other hotspot. It occurred to me that their armor and weapons might be enchanted. And if so, was it possible they did not know or care? The Taurans had said these were a strange and docile people. In fact, during our sea voyage, they had made many derogatory jokes about how unwarlike Paijans were. So, for such a group to be here, wearing clearly enchanted armor… it had to be ignorance. Lovik's words came back to me: *the people do not know.*

Jem came back, held up his hand, rubbed his index finger and thumb together a few times in the universal hand sign for money, and held up four fingers of the other hand. Olimen gave him four gold coins and was clearly not very happy about it. When Jem gave them our money, the one I assume was the leader took them, inspected them quickly, and handed them to one of his men. They seemed pretty amused by the whole thing. He then handed Jem a couple of small objects and waved his dismissal.

When Jem returned this time, he presented Olimen a small ivory or bone pendant carved into the shape of a hand, hanging from a leather necklace, and a packet of waxed paper. As Olimen took the items, Jem spoke in his own language. Olimen nodded in understanding, then looked at us and said, "Jem says we won't encounter any more patrols. This is the military perimeter around the capital. This symbol will grant us passage. Apparently, the patrol captain also believes we are also dressed in too many clothes for how hot it is."

Tomas said, "He's not wrong. Had I known, I would have brought lacquered bamboo armor instead of plate."

The waxed paper envelope contained a fine white powder. It looked like a spice that Jem sprinkled into his dinner each evening. As soon as Olimen opened the envelope, I realized it was the source of the Warp I had been detecting.

Olimen said, "He also says this will help us feel more comfortable in the heat."

I told Olimen about my prayer and the presence of Warp in the powder. Olimen asked Jem a question, and in response Jem began to gesture with his hands, speaking as he did so. First, he made as if he were taking a pinch from the envelope in Olimen's hand, then sprinkling it. Then he made the motions of eating from a bowl, and stopped talking. Olimen said, "Jem says we have it all wrong. It isn't a flavoring, it's a prayer, like the ones we say over our meals. They only do it for the biggest meal of the day."

Jem spoke up again and continued to mime. The invisible bowl was gone and now he was using one hand to pull a glove onto the other. He wiggled the fingers of the hand wearing the imaginary glove.

Olimen listened, then said, "The white hand, that symbol we keep seeing? It's a mark they receive as newborn babies." Clearly sensing the coming questions, he said, "It's only paint. They renew it periodically throughout life, on certain ceremonial occasions or when they're feeling particularly devout. This white powder is a daily reminder of that marking. They call it *The Glove*." With that, Olimen's translation prayer faded, and he apparently didn't see any reason to repeat it. We moved on.

The village ended up being nothing special, at least at first glance. It was glorified clearing ringed by tall trees with wide green fronds like palms, and thirty some buildings, maybe homes. The worksmanship in their stonecraft was apparent but it had been many years since any maintenance had been done. The jungle already creeped in. We saw a few places where someone had painted a bit here and there, but the general disrepair of the village is what stands out in my mind. In a few years, the jungle would swallow them up, and no one would even know. The people, the Paijans, might not even know. At the time, it just added a sense of melancholy to my inner thinking about what had to be going on in Pel Paijan.

The village was small, quiet, and unremarkable except for the fact that we couldn't see any people. In the center of the clearing was a larger building, also cylindrical, with a conical roof. It looked a bit like a dwarven smithy, maybe, even more so because of the white smoke rising from the vent at the top. Since that was the only apparent fire going, I assumed this was a tavern for travelers, or maybe the village hall: after all, a village-wide meeting would have explained the complete lack of any people out and about.

We approached the central building, hoping to find whoever lived here and secure food, lodging, and more information. At the door, Olimen put his hand to the door and looked at Jem. Seeing no indication of alarm or disapproval from our guide, Olimen pulled the door open and we entered.

As I had been expecting the bar and tables of a tavern, or the furniture of a meeting hall, it took me a moment to process what I saw once my eyes adjusted to the dark, smoky ambiance. It was a single large room. The floor was nothing more than worn and filthy reed mats over mud. There were sleeping pallets and cots everywhere, maybe half of them occupied with people sleeping, though it was the middle of the afternoon. On the ground and on low tables, dozens of censers gave out thin white tendrils of smoke that swirled to fill the room, then combined and commingled into the column we had seen issuing from the chimney.

Before my eyes could even finish their report, though, my nose was overwhelmed. I can only describe the smell as an assault. A cloying, heavy smell of burnt sugar, and underneath the sweetness, tiny hints of overripe fruit, of sweat, of wine that's not quite gone over to vinegar that you know you'd better finish or throw out today.

I took a step back out of pure instinct. So did Tomas and Olimen. I pointed to the censer closest to the door and waved for Olimen's attention. It was burning the Glove.

"This isn't a tavern," Olimen said. "It's a shrine. This is their worship. This must be the sugar smell Lovik described." With that, all the mismatched puzzle pieces just snapped into place in my head. I opened my mouth to speak, but I could see that Olimen's thought was already there: *spiritual withdrawal*. Our early guess, improbable as it seemed at the time, had been right all along.

* * *

A larger building with smoke rising from its center passes for the tavern here. We enter it and find muddy floors covered with reed-mats. Sleeping palettes have been lifted off the ground by about a hand's height. Everywhere, incense burns. I tug on Olimen's sleeve and point to one of the censers. It's burning the same white powder our guide used, called the Glove. It smells like sugar. This feels wrong to me and I back out. We all do.

Jem has already hailed the owner – the priest - who picked his way to us through sleeping bodies. We saw what might be adventurers deeply asleep even though it was late afternoon. The shelf full of liquor bottles had a small figurine of a winged serpent painted in gold. I note this to Olimen but he is focused on Jem and the tavern owner.

"This isn't a tavern," Olimen says to me and Tomas. "It's a shrine to this golden serpent god. This is their worship." He sniffed the air. "This is the same sugar smell Lovik described. Their worship is drug-based." The flat tone of his pronouncement struck me as truth. I felt the puzzle pieces of Lovik's early symptoms into withdrawal and death click into place. How did we miss it? We hadn't. We ruled it out because we have not a single record of spiritual withdrawal, or any religion like this, right?

"Somehow, Lovik became addicted to worship drugs…" I restate.

These people used the drugs so casually in the course of their daily lives. "I bet Lovik didn't know they were drugs. Every night, Jem has offered it to us. Without Lovik's death on our minds, we would have taken them out of politeness." I close my eyes. "Lovik was gone for three weeks. Twenty-one days is enough to get addicted to even mild drugs."

Tomas is fidgeting with his sword. "Or, he was intentionally given more potent versions. I can't believe Lovik's death would come from the Glove. Jem uses it the way our lords sprinkle pepper on food. That is to say, not much at all."

Olimen turns to what must be a priest and begins asking questions. Knowing this man is a priest, I pray and my ability to detect evil reactivates. I see more of Warp's power around the man. Not much. If he were a Tiamat priestess, my vision would be full of fire. Tanians do not hide their ambition or violence. I look more closely and note things I did not see before.

The cleric is middle-aged. He is in the prime of his life and at peak physical fitness. He radiates healthiness. His eyes have a glassy sheen to them but the inside is dark. I'm struck by Lovik's reaction to the candle before he passed away. Olimen nods at the priest and walks in. The man beats his chest and points to the various features of the shrine. I can imagine him saying, "We have twenty worship beds in this great shrine…" but it had to have once been a bustling tavern. No one makes taverns out of stone unless they're wealthy and retiring or the tavern is just that busy.

I was so intent on seeing a tavern I missed the prayer cots. They are lined with silk. About half have worshippers on them. Some are sleeping. Others are staring at incense smoke drifting from censers near their heads. While most of the incense sticks seem to wick the Glove drug, some burn other colors. A woman catches my eye. She is pregnant and will soon give birth. She is rubbing a red powder on her belly. She looks ecstatic, like aroused ecstatic. I avert my eyes.

I want to see more, but an aversion has taken hold of me and I cannot find the strength to enter. It feels like sugar is crystallizing in my eyes. Tomas won't go in either. We wait with the horses and I study the village. Everyone seems happy. They are curious about us, but stay away. There is work going on, but it is slow and casual as if the people have not a care in the world. We have drugs like this here in Taysor, but the users become too laconic to work at all. There are many children and I remember the pregnant lady rubbing her belly again.

After an hour, Olimen comes out. His eyes are watering and he looks glazed over. Jem and the priest are looking at him with concern as he staggers over to us. "I know what happened to Lovik." He taps the white hand emblem the patrol guard gave him. "They think I'm a worshipper of the Golden Serpent from a faraway land. They told me that the Hand and the Glove are sacraments. If you don't take them regularly, you go into withdrawals, actual physical and mental withdrawals." His words are a bit slurred. "They all have a tolerance to it that begins with the Birthing Ceremony Lovik went to." Olimen grabs my shoulder. "It's not an illness. It's addictive poison."

His breath is coming in wheezing gasps and I check his pulse. His heart is fluttering. I nod and embrace him, trying to look like I'm giving him a brotherly hug. The village activity has stopped and the Golden Serpent priest is looking at us quizzically. I pray to Pha Rann to expel the poison from

Olimen. My prayer is fast and quietly whispered so that only the high priest and I can hear. The effect is instantaneous.

Olimen drops to his knees and I steady him as he begins to retch. The Golden Serpent priest runs forward. He grabs a small vial containing a red-tinted liquid. My detect evil hymn is still active and I see a higher concentration of Warp in this red liquid. He dabs some on his hands and rubs them together. When it becomes apparent he's going to touch Olimen, I catch his hands. Without my support, Olimen falls to his hands and knees as his body finishes expelling the drugs.

The Pel Paijan priest looks at me wide-eyed and I hear a collective gasp from the villagers. Jem drops to his knees and lifts his hands to the sky as if imploring the gods to do something. I don't understand what happened but it seems reasonable that they're reacting to my stopping the priest. He must be a lot more important than a village priest in Taysor is.

It occurs to me that if I did this in Tania, a paladin would have already amputated my arms. I let the priest go with a smile and a bow. I try to convey my apologies but point to his hands and Olimen. I shake my head firmly and pull a handful of Paijan gold from my pouch. The priest eyes it and asks me a question. He seems confused that we cannot understand each other. I point to my lips and shake my head and then bow subserviently to Olimen. They understand servants and masters and orders.

Tomas has untied the peace cord on his weapon and is eyeing the crowd. His intimidation works well and I thank the Sun that intimidation does not require fluency in foreign languages. The priest seems about to make a scene and then shrugs. He holds his hands up to the sky and calls out to the village. About half of them run forward.

The priest choses a young girl and anoints her crown, temple, and under her nose with the substance. It looks oily to me. Apparently, once it is offered, it must be used. My evil detection prayer shows Warp suffuse throughout her body but only for a few seconds. The residual euphoria she seems to derive from it continues long after.

Olimen has recovered enough to stand and we eye the girl. She shudders and the rest of the crowd cheers when she jumps up and spins in a circle. The euphoric smile on her face, and the crowd's reaction, tells us that this is a much more potent sacrament than the two we'd already encountered.

Jem sidles up to Olimen and whispers urgently. I know it's about the girl, and the priest. "We should leave," the high priest says to us. "It'd have been nice to stop and bathe, but we can't stay. Jem says things will now happen with the crowd and the girl that he thinks will offend us. We will travel all night and reach Pel Paijan tomorrow. Jem also says the priest will report us to the patrol. No one touches the priest except sexually in one of the higher ceremonies."

I almost ask what will happen but when I see the girl gyrating and the leering grins of everyone in the village, I understand. "Yes, let's leave."

Our horses are less indomitable in their desire to reach the capital than we are. We have to pray over them several times. Jem offers to feed them the Glove and we shrug. Since these are Paijan horses, why not? Tomas, of course, is unhappy with this arrangement but Olimen overrides him. We settle into a rhythm and Olimen begins asking Jem questions about other drugs and what they might do.

After several minutes, where Jem grows increasingly agitated, Olimen turns back and explains, "The Hand, the Glove, and that red oil, which they name 'The Smooth,' these are the only ones he knows about. It's very apparent that, where we pray to Pha Rann, they use drugs infused with divine power instead of prayer. The fragments of Warp you see, Jerranic, that is the Golden Serpent's influence in the drugs. The drugs by themselves aren't good or evil; they just are." Olimen sat in silent thought for many long minutes.

I had my own thoughts and Lovik's insistence that the Golden Serpent was not of Heaven kept coming back to me. If not of Heaven, if not the All Father, could it be a corrupted creature of good? I could remember not a single instance of such corruption. Captured, experimented on, killed… yes.

Corrupted? Impossible! The more I thought about it, the more certain I became that the Golden Serpent was a devil, maybe even a Hell Lord in disguise.

Dare I voice it aloud? My whole purpose for being on this mission is my ability to call on Pha Rann in the heat of combat. I was not selected because of my soaring intellect or strategic mind. If anything, I was so enmeshed in tactics…

I hear a sound as if wind moving past me. By itself, it was nothing. But, we were in a thick foreign jungle. Lovik's death lay heavy on me. My dark thoughts of a Hell Lord made me jumpy. I wish I could say my conscious brain registered it as a dart. The truth, as much as I hate to admit it, is that years of training in the Temple and then a brief stint going through what Tania does to their battle priests kicked in. I slipped off my horse as my eyes traced the sound to the right side of the trail behind us.

Tomas startles at my sudden movement and I note a faint sound as another dart bounces off his armor. Adrenaline and battle focus bring a hymn into my mind with sharpened clarity. I can see the key notes of the hymn short cut and summarized. A column of fire bursts forth in the area where the attack might have originated. That's when Tomas realized we were under attack. Though his armor saved him, his horse collapsed to the poison. All around us, padded movement and rustling foliage suggest many attackers. We are surrounded.

Olimen begins a call to remove himself from time and combat. That spell would allow him to see and act with Pha Rann's favor. It is a good support spell. The column of yellow fire has ignited the jungle with light. Amid the cast of dark shadows racing away from the light, I spot at least ten assailants.

Tomas dodges his horse's fall and summons his holy avenger into his hand. In the second light source now, we can see the captain from the earlier patrol and the village priest. They are ringed by a handful of villagers holding spears. A red stripe of paint smears across their faces and I have no doubt the red stripe is a new prayer drug meant for combat.

Multiple puffs sound from all around and darts streak at Tomas. Most glance off his armor, but a few strike his skin. He charges the priest. That priest, so friendly seeming in the daylight, now radiates a sense of menace made worse by the near nakedness of the village men. Spear points glistening with greasy ichor rise up to meet Tomas. Probably yet another prayer drug or poison from the Golden Serpent. I wonder how many drugs they have.

"Pha Rann commands the priest's death!" Tomas shouts this as he steps into the spear points. His plate armor mostly saves him. I wince as at least two stick him through soft spots between plates. Having hit our fighter, the entire unit Paijans falls back. Poison or something indeed. The patrol captain makes ready to throw something at Tomas.

Is that a net?, I wonder. *Oh, I see. The spears, like the darts are poisoned. They're waiting for Tomas to fall. Idiots, this*

Golden Serpent must not have paladins. Tomas' training makes him press forward as the serpent priest's eyes grew wide in disbelief. I admire Tomas in his reckless charge. He feels the poison, or whatever it is. He's ignoring the real wounds. He's right, the priest is the target.

My horse falls and exposes me to the dart blowers. This is okay by me as I now have another prayer rising into my soul. The intricate binding runes and the prayer of holding will allow me to freeze at least some of them. "Paralyze!" I command while pointing my hand at the patrol captain. Tomas can take out the priest easily. A trained fighter might pose a problem. To my satisfaction, the captain freezes in the middle of sweeping the net forward. His halted momentum makes him fall on his side.

My flamestrike and the light of the now burning jungle gives me a perfect view of Tomas, with a spear sticking between his shoulder pauldron and breastplate, decapitating the priest. The flaming sword lopes the shock-stricken head of the priest right off. A normal warrior would pause and savor the kill; Tomas is a paladin. He whirls and the villagers jump back from his burning flame blade. One is not fast enough. At the last instant, he flattens his blade and knocks the villager hard enough the poor man tumbles to the ground and rolls trying to get away.

I feel numerous darts strike me, but I don't care. We had won. Olimen would neutralize the nausea already eating into my stomach. At least it was not a lethal poison. I counted fewer than twenty villagers in the forest around us now. They each hold blow darts and tubes. Apparently, the death of the priest did not demoralize them at all. Maybe it's that red stripe on their faces. I had rather hoped the priest's death would make them all flee.

As they lifted up their tubes and aim at Tomas, I unleashed one of my deadliest spells. At Pha Rann's command, the stones all around them turn to needle sharp spikes. Like thorns but so sharp they cannot be felt except as pain and blood loss. It would slay them all. In my heart, I pray for their afterlives, but without their surrender I cannot wait for them to do the right thing. As one, the group of attackers wilt and die.

Olimen touches my shoulder from behind and heals me while expelling the poison. His faith stabilizes my vision and other senses. Tomas has since slain two more villagers, by accident it seems with the flat of his blade.

We find Jem in a fetal position, rigid and quivering. The poison on the darts, while not lethal, looks painful. When Olimen revives him, Jem begins yelling. At the sight of the decapitated priest and the paralyzed patrol captain, he drops to his knees and pleads to the sky, ignoring us. At last, he points an accusatory finger at us and flees.

My friendship prayer takes hold of Jem a few steps away from the jungle. Though I do not speak his language, I know what he would be thinking: they are my friends, they saved me, why am I running away from them?

I hate this prayer as it twists a person's natural feelings into something not true. It is too close to Warp, but it has its uses. Tomas smirks at me, as if reading my thoughts. He asks me, "What do you want to do with the patrol captain?"

"Our Tanian friends would no doubt interrogate and then kill them," I said. Olimen was prayerfully seeking guidance. It would take him a few minutes. "We can't do that and I can't put all of them under charm."

Tomas shrugged. "They're not a threat for now. I'm going to tie them up and disarm the captain here."
When Olimen at last spoke to us, the survivors were bound and disarmed. "The Sun wishes us to proceed to the Golden

Serpent Temple. We are to ascertain the true deity behind this, capture as many of these drugs as we can, and leave with due haste. The longer we stay, the darker our fate becomes."

His words parted the cloud of battle and left me a surety that we must do these things. I nodded and combined with Olimen as he turned to heal our horses. I pointed to the paralyzed Paijans and gestured for Jem to stay with them all and keep them safe. His charm would wear off about the same time their paralysis would.

With the Sun God shining on us in the jungle night, we galloped to the Golden Temple. We had a fire in our hearts. The attack had clarified our purpose. A dark god lurked in Paijan. The god set itself amidst heavenly trappings. He had priests but they used drugs and poison instead of faith.

We pressed on. We were all used to depravation. Lack of sleep, poison…, we could deal with these for days before actual spiritual fatigue would make us stop. By then, we'd be aboard the Tauran world galleon and away from this narcotic theology. *We should be*, I corrected myself. Lovik had not made it.

The golden spires ignited in the morning light when even the tiniest sliver of light hit them. Despite ominous clouds and gusting winds that grew steadily worse, Pha Rann allowed us to fortify our horses. Without Jem feeding them, our steeds began to show early withdrawal symptoms from the Glove.

Tomas hummed a preparatory war chant. I found myself joining my voice to his and harmonizing. It was a gift from my time training with the Tanians and their worship of Tiamat. I shook my head and scratched at some of the scabs where darts had pierced me just ten hours before. My Order's ancient teachers would not recognize me or our actions. The Merakoran Temple would ostracize us as heretics. That I had joined the Tanians and studied their training methods, had even joined those practices,… it still made me wonder when the Temples would punish me. I remembered the first time I was that close to the Paladins of Tiamat.

They did their combat dance of smashing armor, kicks, and sword movements. Into their midst, a single priest had walked. He was young. Someone told me his name was Tembri. The name, even back then, was whispered with awe. He was the first battle priest to complete a Bloodstone tour. He was the first to earn R'Dar rank. He was the first to be gifted a bloodstone. The powder of that stone made the red dragon tattoo along half his body gleam. He did something I had never seen before: he called a flamestrike and then split it into seven columns to dance and track the movements of the seven paladins.

"How is this possible?" I exclaimed. "Did he trigger seven prayers at the same time?"

Tembri either could not hear me for the roaring of the flames, or chose to not answer me. He joined in the dance. Despite his clear focus on the combat dance, his fire columns remained active; something I had never contemplated before. I watched and prayed to suppress the envy, and fear, kindled in my soul. Tania's beginning as an empire of priestesses and paladins had ultimately made them the strongest nation, perhaps ever. If Tembri represented a new evolution…

Later, I found the Dar priestess who presided over the assembly. "I wish to train with you. I want to learn how Tembri did this."

The priestess, Dar Niss, had some office in their paladins' Order of Fire. I could never tell what it was. She was beautiful, if somewhat past her prime. I had come to expect all Dar priestesses to be immaculate and sensual avatars for

Tiamat but she had age wrinkles. Where most of the transcended priestesses were vibrant and seemingly agelessly youthful in their mid-twenties, Niss appeared almost like a ghost if still young in her thirties. I learned later that she had decided to age and die, what they call 'the dragon's kiss.'

She smiled at me and said, "You are most welcome to, Jerranic." She left a slight pause.

"But? You have more to say, I take it. What is the issue?" I knew she would say because I serve Pha Rann. I prepared myself for a careful and diplomatic argument.

Niss pulled me to her and put her arm around my shoulders. Her nearness was… captivating. In the jungles of Paijan, I shook the recalled scent of her smokey perfume away. It still haunts me after all these years. Tembri's death locked my Tanian memories, forever, in nostalgia.

In predawn, I can feel her lips a hair's breadth from my ear. "You have not passed the rites that would help us understand your own safety in studying these things."

I gulped then, and remembering it now so perfectly, I gulp again with the memory. "My own safety?" I had expected discrimination.

"Yes, all our paladins, all our clerics are power ranked. This is how we know not to put a veteran with an initiate. This is how we know the paladins can endure Tembri's fire." Her fingers caressed my hair and neck. It raised goosebumps along my body and made me ache for things I long gave up in my Order.

"I will do these rites then," I state as confidently as I can. I want to sound strong and sure. Instead, my voice squeaks. It could have become quickly worse but Niss giggled and made it all okay.

That night, Dar Niss and three other priestesses woke me up and rushed me into a rain-soaked courtyard. There, a paladin stood with his sword drawn. Another paladin stood in a similar attitude. Niss shoved me into the courtyard and said, "Your job is to heal them both as they fight to the death. My sisters and I will judge your discretion for how much healing you apply to what wounds. You must not let either die. They will only stop when you are spent. We will judge you on this as well."

The paladins did not look happy to see me, but both bowed to Dar Niss with a haughty look my way as if to discredit my powers as a cleric of Pha Rann.

Their combat began like the basic sword dance I see everywhere in Morbatten. However, with razor swords of flame and sharp shield edges, they quickly began inflicting damage on each other. I moved around their combat looking for tell tales signs of damage. After just a minute, Niss caught my arm and pointed to the shield hand of the knight we stood behind. "That hand sign means he wishes for a prayer that will fortify his hardiness." I nodded but when I began to focus, Niss interrupted me again, "The other is calling for healing. That hand sign means basic healing. He must have been concussed. Jerranic, not all wounds will have blood signs."

Flustered, I tried to bless the one and heal the other… and failed at both.

I am jarred out of my reverie when my horse almost stumbles off the trail. I spy a deep ravine on my left side. Even with Pha Rann's aid, the horses are too far into early withdrawal. Though we have the drugs, knowing now what they are, we cannot – in good conscience – give them to the animals. After I recover my senses, I call out to Tomas and Olimen. They have both outpaced me. "The horses won't last much longer."

Tomas gives me a wave that could mean he understands, he agrees, or hurry up. I spur my horse forward. The next bend in the river shows a mighty bridge of metal cables arcing over the ravine and river. Like everything else here, the bridge shows a scale of craftsmanship I cannot imagine the village priest and townspeople even approaching. It's a sobering thought that they are this oblivious to having fallen so far.

As we draw near, we see a fortified tower and many guards. They look alert but our attention is drawn to the bridge. The cables have been worked to look like snakes coiling upon each other in never-ending braids. Art worked into the scales shimmer with rainbow patterns. The golden sheen of the morning light is clear even though the sun has yet to appear through the clouds. It has a patina that suggests the work is several decades old. However, underneath the veneer I can already see the handiwork of an older construction. This religion must be fairly new, at least in the timescale of the Pel Paijani country.

Rain begins falling when we are still a few hundred paces from the bridge. Olimen holds back so I can catch up. "The guards look alert. Maybe for us. Assume it's for us. I will pray to Pha Rann to mask us in the rain. Tomas, Jerranic, do not engage."

"Yes, high priest," we both reply at the same time. Tomas laughs and adds, "After the distasteful business with that priest, I'd rather relish a fight with proper opponents."

"But, are they evil opponents?" I say to his back.

"At this point, does it matter? They serve Warp." I find myself wanting to offer the Tanian rebuttal. Tanian laws and customs are so strange but make so much sense, especially in a place like this. I can imagine Dar Niss arguing that addiction-based worship defies moral agency and thus the Paijans might be good; or evil. For Niss, it'd be a fun discussion and it would be ended if the Paijans ever took up weapons against her. Maybe Tomas' view, in this regard, is closer to Tania's?

Mist and fog rise up around us. With the rain, the guards would have to bump against us physically to detect us. The tower faces us as we turn left onto the bridge. Someone calls out, "Ho there, we hear horses. Who goes there?"

We do not answer. That same voice orders guards to investigate and we hear them behind us. They say it's nothing.

The bridge is marvelous. Wooden planks soaked in tar make up the floor of the bridge. It is wide enough for four wagons to move across in the same line. I want to look at it more closely because occasional art on the sides catches my eye. A golden serpent carrying travelers across the bridge, people falling from the bridge and being eaten by alligators, and serpent symbols of every kind engaged in generally helpful actions lures me into thinking this is not a Hell Lord after all. I pray and reassess the next section to catch my eye. I notice, this time, the sinister undertones of the golden serpent's bared fangs. All humans are in an attitude of slavish worship. The serpent's eyes feel dead when I look at them, or alien.

When we are safely on the river's other side, and past a similar fortification, I move up to Olimen. "Though they use drugs, their priests are able to communicate with divine messengers, same as us. Hell Lord or not, those guards were looking for us. I suspect the temple and city around it will also be looking for us. I rather wish we had a mage."

Olimen sighs. "I've been thinking on the same thing. When we started, Pha Rann showed me that bringing a mage would result in all of us being captured. Only you and Tomas endure this. This is why I left Vindi behind. Sydney too."

I smile and feel proud to have caught the elder in a similar train of thought. Since my time in Tania, I view the world more competitively. "In Morbatten, I was power ranked at level nine. They recognized thirteen possible levels before the R'Dar rank. For just a moment, I was proud to be level nine. This whole trip, I am proud to serve with you, Olimen."

I don't know why I said that. My recollection of my training, the tension of the bridge, the battle with the villagers, it's making me melancholy. But, the gratitude I feel at Pha Rann guiding Olimen to bring me fills me with hope. "We're going to do this. I've been thinking about strategy."

Tomas has joined us now. "A glorious death here serves no one," he says. "The only strategy – and glory - here is recovering the drugs for study and leaving this hell country."

I ignore his pessimistic tone. I do not want to lose my inspiration and this correct feeling of thankfulness. I explain, "We will enter in disguise. The next patrol, I'm going to charm and they will sell their armor to us for a fair price. I'll send them to aid the bridge guards. We'll march in as if Paijan guards."

Tomas frowns. "I do not like charms. It smacks of evil, but I defer to Olimen."

Olimen nods. "It must be as Jerranic proposes. I have meditated on this for many hours looking for a more direct and forthright approach. Whether we attempt to buy the drugs from the temple or worshippers, whether we assault the temple, whether we stealth into it…, we all get captured. I have shied away from asking about subterfuge for fear you would consider it an order. Jerranic, the god smiles on this approach. We will follow your lead." Olimen sighs. "Our horses will die if we ride them even another hour. Let's continue on foot."

When we dismount, the horses stagger away. Riding them, I did not notice the gradual onset of their palsy. They show the same early symptoms Lovik did. "Someone will find them and give them the Glove," I say. The others nod. It's against our nature to let them suffer and we pray for their well-being. We huddle together and Olimen prays for us. His hands on our shoulders, his words in our hearts, we feel our limbs strengthen and our thoughts clarify. His blessing is powerful enough to banish the lack of sleep and fatigue luring my thoughts into the past, and towards sleep.

From there we run. We find a patrol. There are too many so Tomas lets most of them chase him. Olimen and I catch three we think are closest to our body types. The trade is expensive, but we refuse to use Pha Rann's blessings to beguile any more than is required for this mission to succeed. Watching them run back to the bridge, I pray in my heart to Pha Rann for forgiveness, to allow this one indiscretion for the greater cause… smacks of Tanian philosophy.

Tomas enjoys his chase and returns to us within an hour. "They do not have much stamina. When I left them, they were all licking that Glove powder out of packets. Maybe that's how this all works. Their demon master saps their health and mentalism, like some undead."

We reach the outskirts of Pel Paijan with the moon high overhead. The militia is stirred and on alert but Olimen's translation prayer registers our words to them as their own tongue. They are on the lookout for a mounted group of three foreigners and a treasonous local. They pay no attention to three tired Paijan guards who had to run to the city with news of an attack and three missing guards a five hour's double march to the west and north.

* * *

The Temple of the Golden Serpent, or as Jem and the priest had named it, 'Radiant Spires,' looms before us. The complex is massive on a level I can only compare to the great fortresses in Bloodstone.
When undead labor, titanic structures can be built over centuries, there is no limit to the size of a construct. Radiant Spires is as big as those and exhibits ornamentation in all aspects of its design.

Firelight reflects off gold leaf on nearly every surface. Mirrors dot the structure as well creating rainbow refractions. No space is left untouched by some artwork or decoration. It is breathtaking in its size and ostentatious flaunting of casual wealth and art.

Radiant Spires was clearly made by veteran artists. Gold leaf and a brilliant white silver paint cover the exterior except for rain spouts and angels-in-place-of-gargoyles made of white marble stone. Gold seams run through the marble. Every surface, even the structural parts present bas relief carvings.

Statues dot thirty tall steps rising up to the entrance. The statues show humans in the attitude of praise and worship. Some have wings with angel countenances. Others battle serpents with human arms holding polearms. The serpents are three times larger than the humans and I note that they might be yuan-ti. Of course, I realize now how wrong I was, though the Taurans did inform us that they have an active trade with a yuan-ti civilization near the Paijans.

A muscled priest with a saber held by a sash at his waist stands atop the steps. He looks at the horizon. Six naked women dance around him with offering trays. As we file up the steps, crowded for being so late, we see the nude women are shackled. So that I can understand and save Olimen some of his strength, I enact a *tongues* prayer. It clears my eyes and ears and I read the signs.

Each one proclaims a sin. Theft of food, taking unearned credit for another's work, stealing from an employer, infidelity to a husband, selling the Glove, and wounding a friend show just some of their supposed sins. Another line of naked men and women stand out of the light holding trays as well. I realize they are waiting their turn to dance. A child is hugging woman there and giving her food. It makes me wonder if the punishment is the dancing or the waiting to dance.

Curious to see what happens, I look in the tray of one, selling the Glove sinner, and see a mix of copper coins. On a whim, maybe because she was beautiful, I give her a gold coin. She gasps and begins to sing. She also jumps into my arms and kisses me. "You're my savior. I am yours!" She whirls to the priest and calls out, "The Serpent Lords redeems me of my sin. May I be set free?"

Tomas and Olimen have taken up flanking positions around me. The priest walks over and counts her coins. He nods but catches her hand and puts it in mine. "You owe this worshipper more than gratitude, woman. For your crime, you should be dancing for more than two days, not just my shift. Gratitude!"

The priest then turns his eyes on me. "You have strange eyes, guard. How did you come by a gold coin?"

Though the priest does not seem overly suspicious, I know my answer will mean everything. I pull the woman close to me. "I've been saving it for a wife and working at the Haram docks when not on shift. It has taken a long time. The Glove tints my eyes when I am in rapture. It's an ocean thing."

"You're from the docks? Do you know Captain Tana there? Perhaps you have a letter of recommendation I might see." The priest has taken a key and is caressing the girl as he unlocks her leg iron. She squirms uncomfortably. I can see her reluctance to ruin her chance of freedom. Any questions I have about the goodly nature of this temple are dispelled by the priest's treatment of her. I pray in my heart and Pha Rann tells me that Tana is not real.

I laugh. "Captain Tana! I've never heard of such a one. I did however work for a much less glorious watchmaster. Maybe you've heard of Master Prem?" Like our guide Jem, I had noticed that lower level Paijans had simple one syllable names.

The priest grins and I know I've passed whatever this test was. The chain comes off the girl's leg. "With a gold crown you could marry three of these, except that one. She's already married. May the Golden King shine radiance on your marriage to Hana."

"Thank you, sir. I have doubts I can pleasure one let alone three women. When I am more glorious perhaps." The other women are crowding around me, begging me, and the priest to choose two more. One grabs Hana and begs her, "Please, tell your master to buy me too!"

I watch Hana eye me and then shake her head. She does not want to risk angering the priest. I see fear in her eyes, and it quenches the beggar's hope too. She nods, imperceptibly, and turns back to dancing. These people fear their god, or at least the religion.

It hurts, knowing I can spare them this humiliation but must not. I pull Hana closer to me and squeeze her. It feels uncomfortable and stirs feelings in me that almost takes me back to Dar Niss and the priestesses I trained with so many years ago. If they could see me now! The priest winks and turns back to the dancers, threatening them to leave the newlyweds alone.

The waiting line shows that it is not only women dancing for redemption. Men and children, also nude, wait their turn for absolution. I cannot imagine having to do this public spectacle for minor and major crimes. I kiss Hana's forehead. "Do you have your clothes here? And, I suppose, how do we get you the Glove? I can't have my new bride stealing it again!" I laugh overly loud. Tomas is rolling his eyes.

Hana giggles. "What is your name, my husband?"

"Jerra," I respond. "Please tell me you're not already married."

"So what if I am, Jerra? You're my husband now. And, no. I am not already married."

Olimen and Tomas are carefully flanking me with enough distance that no one notices we make a group. The great doors entering the building form a tunnel. Golden curls of light shimmer as if from a pool of water onto the black walls and ceiling. While black meets my expectations for a hell lord, the beauty of the radiance does not. I feel unbalanced here.

"Hana, my wife, I have never been here. I came to find you. I do not know how to do anything here at Radiant Spires.

Please, pretend I know nothing and teach me as if a child. This is my first wish as your husband. I do not wish to be embarrassed in your eyes."

She swoops in front of me and takes my other hand. I'm staring at a beautiful young and very naked Hana. Any number of holy mantras run through my mind and I force myself to take her all in the way a Paijan might. She exclaims, "Okay, Jera! First, we must go the fountain and make a wish. If our wish is accepted, a servant will bring us the Hand, the Glove, Excite, Incite, whatever you want. We can even get a private counsel with a priest and consummate our marriage here! It all depends on how much gold you have."

She sounds excited. Golden Temple, Golden King, Golden Serpent indeed; I'm noticing a theme.

Fortunately, I have a lot of gold. "I grew up in Pa Haram, working the docks. When I was ten years old, one of the massive minotaur ships arrived. I don't know why, but the Taurans liked me, a lot. They gave me work. When I became a guard, I was able to earn far more. I have a lot of gold, Hana. Pa Haram did not have Excite or Incite. What holy purpose do those have?"

Hana pulls me to her and presses her breasts against me in a spinning hug. I catch Olimen's eyes and see he is struggling to not laugh. He knows my exquisite suffering. Tomas is dutifully not paying attention. We all have the same vows of chastity.

Hana whispers in my ear. "Lots of gold and a handsome husband, can the Golden Serpent bless me anymore? I feel as if my heart might explode for joy, Jera! Excite allows its taker to exert the Golden King's influence on others." She grabs at my groin and rubs me. "If you know what I mean. It excites those around you. I don't know what the Temple's name for it is. The other allows its taker to be excited by others. When taken together, they are named as Shining Rapture." She coils her legs around mine, practically climbing my body. "Imagine two people in the Shining Rapture each wanting, no craving each other's pleasure." She bites her lip. "It's something I've only ever dreamed about. Please, may we do it?"

We continue and enter a great hall. The center of the hall is filled by a statue seven-men tall. It shows a serpent in gold. It resembles a yuan-ti but also does not. Wings rise up from its back and the serpent holds aloft a sheaf of corn. The other holds a chalice. From both pour water into a fountain. Interior light from the water creates the refracting patterns we saw in the passage. In this chamber full of gold and silver, it makes the entire place scintillate. Remembering Lovik's vision pain, I imagine that someone low on the Glove would not be able to enter this place. Maybe it's a test?

Hana pulls me to the fountain and I see piles of treasure in it. A fat man near us eyes Hana with a hungry look. Seeing that Hana is expecting a reaction from me, I glare back. When he licks his lips and makes an obscene gesture, I punch him. I don't want to brag, but I'm as strong as Tomas. My punch somersaults the fat man into the fountain. Hana jumps up and down and claps her hands. Her excitement is becoming infectious and I laugh too.

I almost never laugh in holy (or unholy) places and it startles me. I notice a mist seeping from the Golden Serpent statue. I point to it. "Hana?"

"That's the Glove. It is freely given to any who enter this holy place." A priest has come over and is fishing the fat man out. I notice the priest liberates the man of his coins as he pulls him up to the fountain's edge. The pickpocket is so perfect I am almost caught gaping at it.

Expecting a fight from the fat man, he instead bows to me with respect. "She is your wife. I accede this. She is pretty though. I remember seeing her when I entered and was tempted to add her to my harem."

Hana moves behind me and I feel her lay her head on my shoulder armor. She whispers, "A fate worse than death, fat one."

He does not hear but now the Serpent Priest is eyeing us. "It is not often a guard attacks a worshipper here, let alone a wealthy merchant who is above you in our grand society. What is your name, guardsman?"

Hana pipes up. "My husband, Jera. He came as a pilgrim from Pa Haram."

The priest looks at me for a moment and I realize that perhaps women do not speak for men here. I clear my throat. "Yes. Golden Priest, may I know your name?"

My deferential tone pleases him as does my withdrawing a gold coin from a pouch full of gold. I let it clink on the edge of the pool and then fall into the fountain. He smiles too quickly and says, "I am Belias. You came for marriage, and took a sinner? I'm impressed, Jera. Most pilgrims spend their lust on the sinners and then enter this place seeking guidance in finding a wife. We have many pure ones to choose from today. You've done it backwards! We have many to choose from if you wish for more. Some are even pregnant already!"

The Glove vapor is making me light-headed. No wonder Lovik had withdrawal. I can feel the drug suffusing my entire body. Olimen comes up behind me and calls out. "Friend Jera! I was wondering when you might show up. I have been waiting." His touch sends Pha Rann's light through my body and the clouding effect of the Glove disappears.

"Oli!" I call back and we thump each other's backs. "Meet my wife to be, Hana. Hana, this is Oli. He taught me everything I know about street brawls, and many things about life." I'm trying to stay honest and true without going into difficult details. Tomas is no doubt nearby and keeping track of my dishonest omissions of truth.

Hana stays behind me as if I'm a shield. I turn to Belias. "I have everything needed in my pilgrimage except a few. The minotaur docks have a shrine to the Golden Serpent. Part of my journey, and the Golden Serpent has blessed me with a wife and helper already, is to restock the shrine's cabinets with holy powders. I'm not sure the holy term for what the Glove, and the like are called; I'm just a guardsman after all. They wished for as much Hand, Glove, Excite, Incite, Joy, and other names I can't remember… as this would buy." I fish a small strongbox out of my backpack and open it.

Belias smiles. "We call those the *Six Sacraments*. You must be well-trusted by your priest to have so much coin and to travel so far. Usually, we send out resupply caravans based on need. I was not aware that Pa Haram had run out. Their priest should have sent word. You're sure you need the Glove?"

It feels like a loaded question to me and I bluff. "The priest," and I hesitate before continuing. His name sounds like a corruption of the Hell Lord Belial. "Dishal," I mumble. "He said he wanted the usual stuff. For the first time, the minotaurs had wanted some too. I am not sure, Belias, but maybe they took it all? In my ignorance, I assumed the Glove, but I am not a glorious priest." I shrug and give Belias a look that hopefully conveys my general confusion about higher order Sacraments. "Until you said Six Sacraments, I did not remember that term. Dishal mentioned it only once. But I have this gold for it. I hope it's enough for the shrine's need."

Belias nods. "There is always room for more gold here. The Golden Serpent treasures its yellow light." Two other priests have come forward and they begin counting the coins. "You may have heard the scriptures, Jera... "The yellow light of the eye shines brightest on gold."

I feel Hana shiver. "Some clothing for my bride would be in order too, I think. Do you have a place of clothing? May we?"

Belias points to the public side of the room. A pile of garments there, most likely from sinners, waits for us. I'm surprised to see many fine and well-crafted items. I point to a silk dress and suggest it for Hana. She laughs. "I could never pull that off, dear husband. People would think you my bodyguard."

I pray to Pha Rann and then catch her arm. "Would that be such a bad idea? You should have a bodyguard. What better guard than your husband?" The suggestive powers in my prayer should work immediately. When she blinks and looks at me quizzically, I realize the drugs permeating this place are in conflict with Pha Rann; it's another sign of Warp.

Shaking off my suggestion as strange, she finds leather armor and dons it, then adds a simple but nicely-tailored dress over it. A short sword joins her garb and she spins for me. "A husband who will guard over my body. I like it. Never did I ever imagine that such a fortune would await a girl unable to afford the most basic of sacraments."

Belias joins us and exclaims, "The Serpent blesses you, Jera. Your wife has the wisdom to not take the flashier clothes that would cause problems later, after their owner's penance." Hana curtsies to him. "We have prepared the Six Sacraments for you. Please follow me. You're in for a treat. Normally, only priests are allowed."

Belias takes us behind the fountain where steps lead underneath it. We descend almost a hundred. The stairs are illuminated with mirrors that bring golden and silvery light from the fountain room to this place. I find another room of penitent sinners. Like those outside, these are all naked too. They wear masks over their face and the room is heavy with the smell of chemical powders. There must have been two hundred people working here.

A stone table is set up, each with an empty leather satchel, wax papers, and stone mortars filled with powders. I recognized the Hand and the Glove. Worried it might be a test, I say. "These are the Hand and Glove, right? Dishan seemed to have plenty of that! I wish I understood these things better."

Belias walks around the table and points to each. "Hand, Glove, Excite, Incite, Joy, and Execution: these are the Six Sacraments, Jera. We will remove the Hand and Glove. I checked our records and Excite seems to be the most popular one in Pa Haram. We will give you more of that. Your request to know more is interesting. Do you have interest or aptitude with the divine?"

Two assistants began pouring the powder into wax packets, which they seal with candle wax and place in the leather satchels. Belias continues. "I sense you have a hidden gift to understand." He dips his finger in the black powder he called Executioner and places it under his tongue. "You try."

I don't want to. Every part of me screams, "Don't do it!" I hear the tread of heavy footsteps behind me and give Hana a kiss as a way of seeing what is happening. Ten guards with shields and crossbows resting on the shield edges have appeared. There must have been a hidden room off the stairs we descended. The bolts are pointed at me. I pretend to not see.

"Dearest Bride, remember for me - as if a child. Shall I test my faith with Executioner?"

She shrugs into my kiss. "It's a great honor." She places her hands on my face and kisses me. "It is called Executioner, because the priests use it before executing miracles."

So that I won't think too much about it, I dip my finger into the black powder and place it under my tongue. It's like licking evil. In all my life, I only ever felt evil like this twice. Once was when I served in Bloodstone and went up against undead. Only the most powerful felt anything like this powder. The other was in Tania when I saw an old man, near death, bind himself to a spell that would give up his life force to ensure his wife and family would have enough money to survive after he passed. The man's life burning away into a scroll for something so petty, had nearly driven me insane.

The powder nearly drives me insane. Olimen's anti-poison spell breaks to pieces against it. My thoughts become inflamed with the possibilities of how Pha Rann's prayers could be turned into weapons through this drug. My training to shortcut required hymns reconnects in alien ways and I see it: Warp in the air around me, in Hana, in Belias, and in the workers. Executioner is not just a drug. I realize I have just consumed a hell lord's blood and a single name blasts my soul with surety: Geryon, the Venom God of the Sixth Hell!

I drop to my hands and knees as, like a trumpet in my ear, the name *Geryon* sounds. I'm dimly aware of Hana touching me with concern… and Belias' laughter.

"The Golden Serpent has found a new priest!" he exclaims. Geryon reaches into my heart and suddenly phantasmal claws becomes the sensual hands of Dar Niss. I fall to my back and Hana is in my arms. *Geryon!*, the name blasts my thinking to shreds again. Belias pins me to the ground and Executioner and Incite pour into my mouth and nose. The Sixth Lord of Hell's name is breaking me. I try to call out to Pha Rann...

Belias yells at me, "Say the God's name!"

I'm thinking and praying to Pha Rann. "Geryon..." stammers the name from my lips.

* * *

Tomas filled me on everything that happened next. I wish, my lord, that I might tell this part for myself. I have vague recall of my time under Geryon's thumb. Trust me, lords, from all the times in my life where I have been forced by incentive or threat to do something I did not wish to do, those were nothing compared to the Executioner drug. It burned me, and as it burned, I felt my connection to Pha Rann fade to nothing. In my mind, I understood it like a snake coiling around me. I wanted to leave, to fight it. I could not. I was bound and helpless. There was no gold, no light. Just Geryon's name trumpeting in my ears.

I'm sure you will have testimony from Tomas, but I will do my best to tell this as he and Hana told it to me after. Forgive any embellishments. I'm rather embarrassed and mortified by, well, everything that happened after I had the drugs forced into me.

* * *

"Something's wrong," Tomas mutters to Olimen. "We should leave."

Olimen cautions to wait longer. "We have to. We cannot leave Jerranic here."

An hour later, Tomas points to the entry. Several guards have shown up and they are not letting new worshippers in. He moves to the passage and sees more guards entering. Several portcullises begin closing. "No!" Tomas screams.

Olimen enacts a sanctuary prayer and blends in with those few remaining. Tomas does not. His holy sword crackles to flame and he charges the lowering gates. Olimen is there behind him. He strengthens the paladin with a spiritual cloak to ward off unholy influences like fear.

They make it through the first grate and see the outer doors closing. Guards there, backlit by fires burning outside the temple, hasten to close the doors. Tomas hits the doors and cuts one of the guards down, but the giant gate slams shut.

"Not a good omen," Tomas growls. "We need a way out."

Olimen sighs. "There is no way except recall. Tomas, our mission is changing."

"Good, I hate failing and we are about to fail our original mission."

From the fountain room, I see Olimen and Tomas. Blood squelches out of the closed gate and I chuckle. Their lack of fear and respect for the Golden Serpent irks me. I call out to them in Soran. "Foreigners! Surrender! There is no hope of escape."

Hana is hesitant where she stands behind me. I can feel her exhilaration to be married to me but I can tell I am scaring her; her fright is delicious. Belias goads me forward. "If they will not submit, they must die."

I nod and began summoning the symbols that shape fire into my heart. I have a foggy memory of brilliant yellow fire connecting the rune shape of Heaven to what we call the 'Eye of God.' It fades and a jagged symbol of green fire and black lightning fills my thoughts. I can taste the imminent death of these two strangers. "If you surrender, I will spare your lives. You have no idea the power against you, Olimen and Tomas."

Tomas points with his sword at Hana and I can feel his covetousness. Though their lips move, I cannot understand their words. I hear lightning crackling all around me. Olimen nods and I can hear them conspiring to take my lovely Hana away. "You dare, when I have yet to taste her sweet flesh? Your insults will be repaid in pain."

"Bring it," Tomas shouts back. He raises his sword and charges. For some reason, I could understand him then. It seems the drugs filter out anything that would divert or delay Geryon's purpose.

I'm about to discharge my fire, when Belias stays me. "Let the worshippers slow him down." All around us, the remaining worshippers, like zombies, are moving to intercept Tomas. I see the wisdom in this. A holy paladin would not strike down innocents when far more tempting targets stand uncloaked before him.

"Hail the Golden Serpent!" I exult. *Geryon!* The name resounds in my soul and I feel new spells connecting and reshaping my understanding of Pha Rann in new and more deadly ways. Any worshippers who fall to Tomas will rise at my command. The weak flesh of peasants will become the steel resolve of powerful undead. Though I never actually tested this with the Tanians, Dar Niss guessed I would be able to summon vampires from the dead.

A gentle voice sounds in my ear. It is Olimen. "Jerranic, remember the Holy Sign of Pha Rann. Remember who you are!"

I dismiss the voice and unleash my gathered might towards the stone floor in front of Tomas. He's about to intercept the fugue'd worshippers. A sardonic voice in my mind names them, "Wall of carrion."
The stone ripples and a pit opens to entangle and topple Tomas, my friend. I shake my head at the strange thought of 'friend.' The stone reforms enough that Tomas jumps and clears it easily. The worshippers, I mean – the carrion reach for him, but are too laconic to grab hold of the armored knight.

His burning sword strikes at Belias. The large priest moves aside and just barely dodges. I want to help Belias. I want to help my friend Tomas. I want to run. I want to serve Pha Rann... no, *Geryon!* The name reasserts itself in my soul and I scream in agony.

Belias might be a better warrior than Tomas but without armor, he quickly receives enough wounds that I reach out to heal him. My spells stutter and do not heal as much as they should. Flashes of Tania come back to me. "Level Nine," Dar Niss said. "Is the ability to heal nine critical and life-threatening wounds. If you do not, the wounds will kill your patient eventually. They have exactly however much air is in their body and blood to act before they die. Our paladins train to understand this and fight through impending death."

Tomas is not injured. Is it fascination that makes me hesitate? I see a burning sun cut through by right angles. It is yellow and white and bright. The shimmering of the fountain's light seems dim and sick by comparison. Why do I serve Pha Rann? *No, GERYON!*

Tomas sweeps his sword to drive the guards now arriving at the top of the steps back. His next strike catches Belias' sabre against his shoulder. I see the blade cut through the armor and blood.

Belias laughs and gloats. "Die, foreigner!"

"Not today," Tomas grunts. The paladin of Pha Rann took the sabre on purpose to open the priest up to counter-attack. Tomas' flame sword pierces Belias' sternum and blows cauterized gore out his back.

The crackling of burning spine fills the room and suddenly, my thoughts are cleared.

Though Geryon's name still shrieks for attention in my thoughts, Pha Rann shines with a brightness that rekindles my own spirit. Hana has the satchels with the drugs. I take her hand and smile. "Come, my bride. It is time to leave. Are you up for an adventure?"

She smiles and squeezes my hand. "I'd go anywhere with you, Jera."

"Tomas! Let's go. I have what we came for."

He begins to retreat, clearly unhappy about it. My *flamestrike* prayer ignites the air and fills the chamber to its ceiling where it spills out and begins to burn the painted murals there. I call to Pha Rann for leniency and twist the prayer so that the column of fire divides in two. Spinning in random patterns, the columns of fire will protect our retreat.

Suddenly, I'm looking into Olimen's eyes. He smiles at me and Tomas. "My dear friends. My beloved students. The time has come to say goodbye."

"What? No..." I protest. Olimen's hand on my chest and the power of his *recall* hymn throws me from the Temple of

Geryon. Hana's fingers in my own threaten to slip and then we fall onto the Tauran world galleon at Pa Haram. Three minotaur guards watching our recall area spin about, weapons ready, and then chortle to see me. They ring a large bell that clangs loud enough to be heard for miles. A moment later, Tomas appears.

"No, Olimen!" Tomas is shouting. "Night take me! My life for you!" Tomas screams for our mage. "Vindi! I need you to send me back! Send me to Olimen! Vindi! Get up here or I will haunt you forever!"

Vindi comes sprinting up to us. Whether drawn by the commotion or by the minotaurs sounding the bell, I wish I knew. "Where's…" he begins to ask but Tomas grabs his cloak and shoves him into the circle.
"Olimen. Teleport me to him, now! That's an order!" Tomas is holding his sword and burning with enough Pha Rannic heat to drive the minotaurs back a few steps.

Vindi nods and begins casting a *scrying* spell. After a moment, he says, "I've found Olimen, I think. Is he in a large golden temple-like building?"

"Yes, yes. Send me there," Tomas is pleading in his urgency.

Vindi begins casting another spell. I recognize the *teleportation* enchantment. I also notice that Hana is standing behind me in a rictus of fear. Her eyes are darting all about and she is clearly terrified by the minotaurs.

"Hana, I'm sorry." I turn around to face her and my sleep prayer collapses her into my arms. I wave a Tauran over and ask him to put her in our quarters, door locked. The Tauran frowns at me, but takes her.

To my side, Vindi touches both Tomas and I. We should blip off the ship and reappear at the Temple. I feel what I think is the beginning of the spell's effect and then nothing. Nothing at all happens. Tomas is about to explode. "Peace, Brother Tomas. It is warded," Vindi explains while smacking his head. "Of course it is. Just like our Temples and the Tanian Temple, it is blocked from teleportation magic."

Tomas drops his sword on the deck and falls to his knees, facing the sun. He begins to pray for Olimen. I feel the same despair but instead ask Vindi to show me Olimen. The mage nods with a heavy sadness. The Tauran Captain arrives and asks what is going on.

When I explain it during Vindi's preparations, Captain says, "I too would like to see this. Though we have traded with the Paijans for many decades, we have never interacted with them in confrontation. They all shy away from it. It makes them profitable but strange."

We go under a large tarp. In the shade, the galleon's mage calls up pool of water on the stone deck. Vindi pours his scrying magic into the pool. A Tauran mage joins Vindi and sound fills the image we see.

Olimen is watching Belias, who has changed. Snake scales dot his body in golden flecks and he slithers forward. Again, it's similar to a yuan-ti but different. The guards who accosted me in the drug refinery are moving forward. When they are in range, they fire their crossbows. I see Olimen smile and change the bolts to snakes. By the time the snakes hit him, they have fallen under Pha Rann's sway and turn to attack the snake priest.

The guards recoil from the serpents, but Belias ignores them. He slithers forward, clear in his intent to charge Olimen. The high priest touches the great gates at his back and the doors twist and warp. The stone frame holding the doors cracks apart and allows sunlight to stream in.

Captain points to the snakes and says, "Using their own imagery against them, tactically sound approach." Another minotaur, who I remember as being important but unnamed says something in their language and they both laugh. Captain translates for us. "He says nullifying the crossbow bolts with snake magic is strong. Like one of us. We did not think you humans, especially of Pha Rann, had this in you."

Belias seems to hesitate at the sunlight's edge and I realize Olimen is purifying it into a weapon. The high priest curves his finger and calls out, "Belias, fight me where your worshippers can see what the Golden Serpent really is! Pha Rann's light will reveal the truth of this for all to see!"

I have never been so proud of my high priest, my friend, as when he walks out to the naked sinners. At his command, their shackles break apart. "You are free of this sham penitence. The Golden Serpent is a Hell Lord, Geryon! Unless you wish to spend your lives in slavery, leave now. Better yet, behold the true face of your god… and rise up. Resist!"

Tomas is still praying tearfully but watching too. "Come back to us, Olimen. Now. It's not too late. Recall, please. Recall."

In my heart, I know he could. I could even send a holy messenger urging this. But, I know my master. He is going to make a stand. "Tomas," I say putting my hand on his shoulder. "Olimen is going to have a glorious death. We are called to witness Pha Rann's defiance against Geryon."

Tomas wipes his nose and calls out, "I should be there with him."

Captain nods. "Yes, you should. Why aren't you?"

Tomas blinks and stares at Captain. The Taurans are so literal. "He sent me back here."

"Then, honor him by standing firm and witness his death. This is his destiny. We should all be so honored by our gods to stand in their holy places, armored with their names. Bapthomet be with him."

Captain's words carry a wisdom I did not expect from the Taurans. The irony of invoking one hell lord's support against another is not lost of me or Tomas.

As the minotaurs in hearing distance make their god's holy hand sign, I pray for Olimen. "Pha Rann, let the sun shine on Olimen. Consecrate his feet to thee. Let his light illuminate the world for ages to come. Let Geryon know that Good stands in opposition even here in Paijan."

Olimen used Belias' hesitation to walk out onto the steps. He turned and faced the Temple. Behind him, the dawning sun had finally risen enough that the entire orb stood free of the jungle mountains. Olimen began to glow as if becoming a second sun. The scrying pool pulsed and ripples shook its surface. The feeling that came with the disturbance raised the hackles on my neck. I glanced at the Taurans and noted their fur stood as is electrified.

"What is that feeling?" Tomas asked.

"Evil," I answer. "Geryon's evil. He wishes to be the Golden Serpent for these Paijans, but he is the Lord of Venom."

Captain nods. "We all stay clear of that one."

All around Olimen, the statues carved in attitudes of worship jerk to life. Their animation reminds me of a reverse poisoning. Black lines of power move through a single 'bite' point and then from there, they begin to move. The winged serpent men that reminded me of yuan-ti lurch to action and move to attack Olimen.

It's too late though. The brilliance of Olimen's faith burns in a circle around him. Compelled forward, the statues burn within twenty paces of Olimen and are stopped as their magic is nullified. Again, our pool ripples with dreadful presence. When it clears, we see Belias, much enlarged, slither forward to strike at Olimen with a giant sabre.

Olimen moves to block it. Not until a strike occurs does Olimen's rod of sunlight become visible. It slags the sabre blade and forces Belias to retreat. *No, not retreat*, I realize. The serpent tail flicks living sinners and statue forms alike at Olimen. The forms tumble through the air and begin landing all around. They burn and Belias cackles as they die. "You let innocent humans die, priest?"

The voice is not Belias'. It is Geryon or something of Geryon. Olimen opens his other hand. A book of Pha Rannic scripture appears there and I recognize our Order's holiest writ. And, I know what will happen next.

"Goodbye, dear friend," I whisper.

Tomas grabs me to ask what but the image of Olimen smashing his rod of daylight onto the cover of the scripture interrupts him. Even the Taurans wince. They must have seen the bloodstone ruby on the cover of the book. I hear Olimen's voice in my soul as explosion and red fire fills the scrying pool. "Take the drugs back to the Temples. We must find a way to free these people and avoid Lovik's fate for them all. I foresee a day when this fell religion will come to the Isles. This is my last command."

Captain must have heard it too because we both acknowledge it as primordial energy fills our scrying pool.

I've never seen a bloodstone destroyed, but the craters along Taysor's eastern quarter still bear testament to what happens when their enchantments are released this way. The galleon's mage pulls us all back as even the pool of water boils to dry vapor and is gone.

Our next scrying attempts are blocked by continuing explosions. Only when Vindi and the ship's mage consult and scry from a farther distance do we see. The façade of the Golden Temple is gone. The tall steps are gone. The upper edifice has collapsed forward. All around Olimen, as debris falls into a spherical fireball, it slags and is jettisoned out. We watch an arc of energy undercut buildings across the street. All around the Temple and within the main structure itself, smoke billows. The city is burning outwards from the explosion.

I imagine I can hear dying screams. I shunt it out of my thoughts. Our order cautions against this kind of indiscriminate destructive violence. Pha Rann whispers peace to my soul. I pat the satchels of the Six Sacraments and vow to understand them.

Around us, the port city of Pa Haram rings out as alarm bells sound. Captain looks out and smiles. "It seems Pa Haram wishes to capture us. By Bapthomet, let us be done with this cursed place. Crew! Prepare to depart! Soldiers, if any of these zombies touch my ship, you are to kill them and ten of their fellows. Decimation orders! Defend the ship!"

Stonemasons across the ship touch the stone deck and bring up siege weapons onto the deck. Within minutes, the cargo carrying ship bristles with weapons. The Taurans, always armed, don armor and even more weapons. The city alarms are for us. Under my feet, the world galleon heaves as weather magic begins to bring us a storm. I feel my heart lighten from the darkness of Olimen's death. Tomas is not recovered.

"Tomas, it is not a sin to destroy great evil. Olimen sent a message that we must follow. This may be the greatest evil we will ever see. Take heart." My blessing soothes his concern and he nods with grim determination. "Go and stand for Pha Rann with the Taurans. I am going to secure the drugs in case we are boarded."

I eye the minotaurs all around us and remember they worship a hell lord often aligned with Geryon. I send Tomas a holy messenger. I tell him: OR THE TAURANS DECIDE TO SELL US OUT.

* * *

I was not there when we left. I was below deck ensuring the Six Sacraments would be safe, and hidden. Though I trust the Taurans to a point, they also worship a Hell Lord. Who knows what plots might occur between two such dark masters as Geryon and Baphtomet?

Later, I heard about it though and wished I was. Apparently, a Geryon priest came in his trappings of heavenly good. He brought a mob of citizens with him, and a few actual guards. Captain walked out on the loading ramp and stood just off the pier. "Any of you dare touch my ship and you will all die. What do you want?"

One of the guards tried to walk up and stand toe to toe against Captain. As the guard took a breath and was about to speak, Captain bit the man's head off and spit it back at the priest. The headless corpse, missing part of its shoulder fell to the side and into the increasingly choppy waters. Everything was silent and then the other Tauran officers dispatched a fire ballista directly into the priest's entourage.

One of the guards shot Captain. It was probably an accident. I'm told he pulled the poison bolt out of his leg and licked it before ordering Pa Haram razed to the ground. "Leave a smoldering pit. I want these monkeys to remember us, forever. No one attacks us, for we are the predators here."

I hastened to secure the drugs and then blessed their hiding place. In theory, only I would be able to find it. I left a note for Tomas in case something happened to me. Hana remained unconscious.

When I arrived above decks, the ship had just barely risen from the muck in the dock area and waves were sweeping the pier. Tomas was pinned by two minotaurs who enjoyed his screams that they not hurt the citizens. It was a mess. World galleons carry a contingent of mages to control the weather and priests to help with everything else. Bapthomet may be their god, but the oceans are their true religion. The people of Pa Haram had no chance. A smoldering pit... I do not doubt Captain's orders were carried out.

Speaking to my concern of how hell lords might ally, I recognized the galleon's weapons as Tanian siege machines. These weaponized golems had but a singular purpose: load and fire. In the distance, smoke rose in streams throughout the city within range of these weapons. The clerics and mages augmented the missiles for extra range and damage. The priest of Geryon stood, reanimated by one of the Tauran clerics and turned to attack the Paijans fleeing the docks.

With ash and ember in my face, stinging my eyes, I realized Pa Haram had become an actual hell. All around me, the Taurans cackled gleefully as they shot harpoons into the fleeing humans. Those speared were dragged back until a cleric could reanimate them. Many of the harpoons, designed to spear whales, pierced many humans.

Remembering Lovik's death, I heard Dar Niss' whisper in my ears… "Better sudden death than the slow death and tortured afterlife Geryon offers those who worship him. Most of them do not even know. It's deliciously evil." Though Niss had never said anything like this, I wiped my eyes and knew that if she were here, she would say it. It was probably an after affect from the drugs I had consumed and breathed in at their Golden Temple.

Vindi came to stand next to me and the Taurans snorted at us in disgust for not helping. Maybe they thought we were too weak to help them. It did not matter. Without Olimen, with drugs still in my system, I did not feel the righteous indignation that would prompt action in this case. To our north, a cyclone was taking shape. Its rotational winds would soon catch our sails and pull us away from this cursed land. While the rain would quench the fires, the winds would first ensure more of the city burned. The artillery barrage from the galleon continued unabated even when we were far enough away that I struggled to make out individual shapes.

"Vindi, when we come back, we will return ready to fight this cult of Geryon." My words sounded right – strong. My heart remembered how powerful the Hell Lord's presence in my soul had been. With atonement on my mind, I went to free Tomas and consult with a fellow tortured soul. The paladin would feel our lack of resistance to this nonsensical violence and genocidal attack much worse than I.
The first smattering of rain fell and began to wash to burning soot of atrocity from my skin.

ERIC K. BARNUM

CREATION
THE BLUE SUN STAFF

Lionel puffed out his chest and looked around the giant courtyard in the middle of The Temples. The Imperial Palace of the Sun gleamed at the end of the northern boulevard. The rising sun peeked through the eastern towers and spires of the Literalist Order of Pha Rann. Scintillating light glimmered along the polished surfaces of plate armor arrayed all around him. It was exactly like he always imagined it would be.

He felt a pride he struggled to put a name to. As a new member of the Holy Order of Cuthbert, Lionel could feel the holy presence of the paladins all around him. While some, like the Pragmatists, had a lighter and more casual feel, the absolute righteousness of Lionel's fellow Cuthberics reassured him that he had made the right choice in joining this Order. "Praise the God Saint," Lionel whispered somberly, a grin curling his lip.

His captain, a middle-aged knight named Ives Smithson, sat atop a large war horse. Pinions snapped in the wind and Lionel wondered if the wind had been conjured to bring the cool air he felt in spite of the day's heat. *That would be just like the Pragmatists, to use magic to make this parade more bearable*, Lionel thought.

He immediately chastised himself. Cuthbert was a bright god, but one in whom there was no tolerance for evil… in any form. "Pride is a poison that leads to bitterness," Lionel recalled from one of his earliest lessons. The instructor, a bent old man covered in battle scars, had lectured them all. "It's not that you're just better than other paladins. Verily, you are! Rejoice! But temper that with the certainty that the God Saint expects more from us. If the other Orders fail to sense their own lacking, that is their sin. Do not compound it by feeling pride at their lack. Accept it as Truth. We are the Sword of the World. Cuthbert will judge us not by how we are compared to lesser Orders, but by how we are compared to our perfect design – the perfect paladin – the perfect avatar of the God Saint himself in this fallen world."

Maybe sensing Lionel's inner mind, Bright Captain Ives looked down at him and said, "Peace, Brother Lionel. Cuthbert requires an ardent and unwavering will. We must judge ourselves by ourselves and for ourselves. Only the Bright God Pha Rann can hold the others accountable for their own lights." Several knights around them bowed their heads and whispered "Peace and Light." After a moment of silence, Ives added, "And yes, the Pragmatists are using magic to create this breeze. Otherwise, we would all be sweating."

Lionel wanted to ask how Ives had known, but mentally pushed the question aside. The motto of the Holy Order of Cuthbert ran through his mind: *By many swords is Evil vanquished.* He forced himself to recite the mantras of Cuthbert. *You are never alone in the Cause of Good*, was his favorite. When he had arrived in The Temples as a fifteen-year-old, he had certainly felt alone. He glanced over to the large central fountain that ringed the statue of a golden woman holding aloft the sun. In any sunlight, the statue's globe burned like the Daystar itself.

With nothing else to do but wait for orders to march, Lionel let his thinking return to that time. He had woken up one night, during a thunderstorm. A voice had compelled him to leave his family's ramshackle hovel in the western province of Otavia. Without understanding why, he had prayed to Pha Rann while racing about to wake his family up and get them out of the house. Though his father had cuffed him, hard, for waking everyone up after a hard day, Lionel had insisted. His faith was next sorely tested when nothing happened for nearly an hour. With his siblings and parents increasingly angry, Lionel had held his ground.

Lionel's faith had proven correct. When it came, it came as a stampede of giants being chased by a Cuthberic war party. The giants had torn through their small home. The paladins on their resplendent war horses had charged through the remnants of broken wood, and dented cooking ware.

Out of the entire village, only their home had been destroyed. Lionel knew, when he saw the strange banners of the paladins, that somewhere a god was watching out for him. Turning to his shocked family, he had said, "See? I told you." It was not just his imagination that the embattled paladin captain, fighting against the giants, had winked at him. He remembered the heraldry banners mounted to the back plates of the knights' armor. The symbol of Pha Rann, commonly called The Eye of God, had been prominent and white with a shield and two crossed swords to either side of the White Eye, as Lionel later learned what they called it. The knights had commended him for his faith and action in saving his family. They told Lionel to turn in the dead giants for bounty and rebuild his home. It should have been enough, but with the money, his father had turned to drink. *I still feel shame for leaving my mother and siblings with that drunkard*, Lionel acknowledged. *When this is over, I'm going home to set things straight.*

"Who are you?" Lionel had called out. "What is your name?"

"I am Ives, younger brother to the God Saint Cuthbert. Come and find me when you are ready."

That was years ago, but Ives had hardly aged. The knights had looked so glorious riding off. The knights could have taken the bounty. *The Pragmatists would have!* Lionel shrugged the thought away and wondered where the bitterness at the Pragmatists came from. *Peace and Light…*

The mantra and focus on the memory of the paladins riding away made Lionel smile. He lifted his face into the sun and took his helmet off. Many of the knights were enjoying the breeze through the courtyard. The sun warming their skin felt like pure worship and Lionel felt Pha Rann's blessing even as the warmth stirred Cuthbert's desires to become holier. Captain Ives took his helmet off too. A perfect silence fell on the courtyard, with even the Daystar Fountain seeming to go still. Lionel felt something malignant move and looked south.

To his right, a darkness crawled along the mountain horizon and reached out towards Taysor. The entire host of all The Temples turned as one to face it. The dark blur became a silhouette staining the sky with red fire. The flames lazily crawled along the thunderclouds blanketing the Shield Mountains. Too far away to see it clearly, Lionel felt the sun on his face grow chill and he snapped his helmet back on and began to pray for wisdom and power to endure whatever trial this might portend.

A voice thundered from the south. It sounded like the storm that destroyed his home and then Lionel realized what it was. He was feeling dragonterror, and had been for some time. That was why his memory had been of his family resisting him, of the giants versus the paladins. It was usually a happy memory, as it had set Lionel on the path to serving the God Saint Cuthbert. Even in the moment of remembering, he had wondered why he focused in on his father and family's resistance, and how they had beaten him, how poor they were.

Captain Ives spoke quietly but with a commanding voice that carried throughout the Orders. "The Tanian dragons are coming, just as High King Andrew said. We are to stand our ground. Supreme Leader Golcir orders that we are to stand and march under the High King's banner. However, five of you are chosen by the God Saint for a different mission. Now stand your ground and pray, all of you. While dragonterror is not itself evil, the Tanians most certainly are. Show them your true mettle!" Captain Ives raised his voice so it boomed out over The Temples. "We serve Creation! Stand at attention, and may Good watch over us all!"

As if wanting to quell Ives' voice, a dire sound rumbled again and vibrated Lionel's bones. Still so far away that he could barely see dark shapes in the sky, Lionel wondered how the dragonterror could be so powerful from so far away. The entire city must be feeling it too, and they were not trained fighters. Captain Ives whispered the truth: "It's the fire dragon king, Alerius."

The red dragon ruler of Morbatten called out and the thunder across the Shield Mountains resolved to their understanding. It said, "We march on Bloodstone to slay the Jade God. We call on Taysor as the Shield, to join us against this great evil. All holders of bloodstones are commanded to join. If Taysor and its militaries shirk our ancient treaties, if the wielders of bloodstones refuse this request, we will defeat the Jade God and then we will burn Taysor to molten dross."

Captain Ives growled at the evil creature's words. He commanded, "Stand your ground! We have our orders from the God Saint himself. We will walk a different path to Bloodstone. Taysor will not burn! We take the Jade God, and if we must, we slay the dragons!" All around, Lionel noticed the other Orders struggle with the fire dragon's demand.

Far to the east, a blinding flash of light ignited brighter than the sun. No sooner did Lionel realize the explosion must be in the City of Ymac than a blast of sound and a shockwave through the stone hit him. The blinding light was an explosion, he realized. A bloodstone had been detonated. He looked to Ives and saw the Captain kiss the bloodstone on his holy avenger's hilt guard. From the east, fire bells and alarms rose up. Two more, smaller detonations, or maybe they were farther away, blossomed against the south and southeastern horizons.

The dragons were close enough that Lionel could now make out their individual shapes. His blood ran cold at the sight of so many. Like frigate birds, griffons flocked around the titanic dragons. Many of the dragons held mighty devices in chains dangling from their claws. Of the group, one led by a dragon larger than the others banked towards them. The ashen scales lit by ember cracks were barely visible through plate armor adorning the Fire Patriarch. The spiked armor polished to mirrors made the fire dragon gleam with ruby light.

Dragonterror hit them again as a secondary shockwave from Ymac made the ground shudder. The dragon's voice came sinister and dire this time. "There is no cause more righteous than ending the Murder of Undeath that is the Jade God. Tania calls on all free peoples - to you, fighters of Taysor - to march on Bloodstone!" As fire breather wheeled around the perimeter of Taysor's walls, Lionel saw priestesses and mages sitting on the dragon's back, and paladins. It was a dark and terrible sight to compare against the might of Pha Rann assembled in The Temples all around him. The fire breather carried at least as many warriors as stood assembled around him in The Temples.

Lionel felt small and insignificant in that moment. "I worship the Sun," Lionel whispered.

Ives replied, "And they worship slaughter. But, in this case, the wyrm speaks some truth. To end an abyssal evil is something we must be a part of. And, our Supreme Leader has a plan to ensure it happens! Order of Cuthbert, draw your swords! Let's show this devil dragon the power of God!" As one, the Cuthberics drew blade and ignited their weapons and armor with brilliant golden fire. Around Ives and some of the veteran Cuthberics, radiant wings swept up around them. In answer, Alerius breathed out flame over the city before breaking his circle over the city's walls and heading west, to the Valley of Bloodstone.

As one, the Cuthberics turned south to exit The Temples to march on Bloodstone. A feeling in his heart held Lionel back and he knew he had been chosen. As Ives passed him by, the Captain tapped Lionel's shoulder armor with his radiant sword. "May the God Saint bless and protect you, Sir Lionel. You are never alone in the cause of Good."

"May Righteous Might Prevail!" Lionel shouted back. It took three hours for the hundreds of paladins and their entourages to empty the massive courtyard. But, within minutes, Lionel knew who the other four were. He knew them by reputation. That they were veteran to him did not faze him at all. One, Supreme Leader Golcir's Right Fist, would be the one to tell them of their quest. Lionel could barely contain his excitement.

When the grand courtyard at last quieted, Lionel walked toward the Right Fist and dropped to his knee. The cleric stood tall in light plate armor. Due to the man's advanced age, the armor was mostly decorative to save on weight, but its emblems noted his many feats. With admiration, Lionel noted fifty winter wars against Morbatten, thirty devil slayings, and ten Righteous Feats. The Feats, for humility's sake, were not stated but were reserved for such mighty acts of valor that they went unsaid during the hero's life. "Righteous Fist Kristof," Lionel said bowing with his hand over his heart.

"Sir Lionel, I welcome a chance to see the valor of a new convert. Welcome." Kristof bowed in turn to the other three. "Well met, my lords and lady. Lionel, this is Lady Hana." Lionel almost blurted out that they knew who she was, but caught himself and bowed to her. Kristof explained, "She began her journey to Cuthbert as a mage and now serves as a priestess to the God Saint. This gives her a unique perspective. While you might know of the other two, humor me. This is Under Captain Petros, and that is Sir Walter. Let us will retire to our Temple and discuss the Supreme Commander's orders."

With every bit the same formality as the paladin ranks marching to Bloodstone, the group of five marched back to the Temple of Cuthbert. It rested between the Perfectionist Temple and the Imperial Palace of King Andrew. As they marched, word reached them that a rogue with a bloodstone had tried to hide it in Ymac. A crater of burning fire nearly two hundred paces deep had destroyed ten blocks of the Northtown slums. Two other stones had detonated in noble residences, though with not nearly the same destruction. The courier speculated that the nobles had forgotten or had not known they had bloodstones.

Once inside the Temple, Lionel felt better able to focus on the end game. While part of him wanted to race west to Bloodstone or east to Ymac and help, he knew that his calling as a paladin meant keeping his eye on the greater prize. "I've been chosen," he said reverently to himself. Dealing with an artefact hidden from the Tanian dragons by an evil rogue was not his crusade. The Right Fist and Lady Hana held his destiny now.

Attendants had already set the room for them. A map of Bloodstone nearly ten paces long and eight paces wide had been rolled out and weighted down with statues to prevent it rolling back up or blowing in the wind. Lady Hana pointed to this and waited for them all to be able to see the map clearly. "I'm going to cast an illusion spell to help explain our mission. Golcir personally chose each of us. He sends his regrets that he cannot be here to bless us himself. Ours is a special mission to ensure his succeeds. To quote him, 'If you succeed Lady Hana, we will most likely meet in person in the strangest of faraway places.' May the God Saint watch over him."

She shook her hands out and then began to cast a spell. With each word, parts of the map became three-dimensional until Lionel could see the mountain heights. The dark red temple of Tiamat at the Second Fortress occupied the center of the map.

As other details filled in, Hana began to speak to them. "Our mission is simple and beautiful in its design. Golcir does us great honor to give it to us. Our objective is clear. We are going to resurrect the Vampire General Crea. Assuming Morbatten defeats the Jade God, we will have but a few moments where, with the entire dominion of Necromancy in disarray, we can recapture one of the greatest clerics of Pha Rann to ever walk the lost civilization of Merakor. The Lord Priest Crea Halavari has walked in darkness too long, nearly four thousand years if the Merakoran histories are correct. We will remind him of the Light." At her words, the three vampire generals appeared on the map in the Temple of Tiamat.

The Right Fist pointed to the three vampires and explained, "Dar Ana alleges it was in 400 DAR, so fourteen hundred years ago, that she liberated the three vampire generals from the Jade God. Those three built the undead armies that in turn built the massive fortresses of Bloodstone. Crea and the other two helped Dar Ana liberate Bloodstone from the Jade God. If Morbatten seeks to slay the Jade God, and succeeds, Golcir thinks it probable that these three will vie to take the Jade God's place in the dominion of Necromancy. If we can get even one of them, it will prevent this from happening. The Tanian dragons talk a good story. 'Hoo ra!' they say. 'Let's defeat the Jade God!' But, the true motive here is that they wish to depose the Jade God with one friendlier to them: Nientro. Crea is our target. If we reclaim him to the Light, we can defeat Nientro. Malcolm will not fight against Crea. Even in Dar Ana's record, it is noted that Crea is the equal of Nientro, if the Jade God had ever allowed it."

Crea's image rose up from the illusion. Hana pointed at Dragon Mountain in Morbatten. "With the Jade God in Bloodstone, Morbatten will not risk the three in that valley. They will either be in Temple at Morbatten or somewhere safe. We suspect the red dragon's secret lair as the likeliest place."

Kristof held up his hand for silence. Though no one said anything, it was clear to Lionel that Kristof expected questions. Only when none came did he say, "Our leader, Golcir, has obtained a way for us to find the vampires. They will, no doubt, be scrying the battle and looking for the right moment to enter Bloodstone. Lady Hana?" An illusion appeared over the Temple of Cuthbert. It showed a staff. A vine twisted around it that opened to flower petals where each flower's center held a sapphire gem instead of a flower.

Petros and Walter both gasped and Lionel suffered for his own ignorance. "What? I assume this is a staff of some importance? Apologies, but I do not..."

"It is the Blue Sun Staff, a gift from Pha Rann to the archmage Galthrest when Merakor at last knew of the Drow threat," Kristof explained.

Petros reached out to touch the illusion. "I've heard that it allows you to see the world as Pha Rann sees it. All truth, as designed, in its perfection. And sin, the darkest stains..."

Hana nodded. "The staff is a marvel of an age where Good held sway and the creation of artefacts like this was much easier than it is now. The archmage Galthrest wrote that the Nexus of Creation was originally blue, not gold. Something about the color of light in a world full of life."

Kristof reached his hand into the illusion as if grabbing the staff. "This is an artefact of immense power. It defeats hidden secrets. Anything touched by its light is confronted with the flaws in its design. It sees the world, and by extension all of us, through the lens of Pha Rann's design. To hold this staff is to know the heart of God. I understand it can be both intoxicating and terrifying. For us, we will use it to know where the three are, and to resurrect Crea."

Walter asked, "So, we'll find Crea with this staff and resurrect him. You're right. That seems straightforward enough. We'll see them with the Blue Sun Staff. Lady Hana will teleport us in. What am I missing?"

Kristof began to answer but Petros laughed. In good humor, he answered Walter. "Nothing! Everything! The other two vampire generals and whatever guardians might be with them will face us. Nientro is essentially an unascended god all by himself. We are but five. In our favor, all eyes will be fixated on Bloodstone. This plan is genius. I can feel the God Saint's approval! We reclaim a fallen son to the Light and defeat god-like evil. I love it!"

Lionel pointed at the illusion of the staff and meekly asked, "This plan hinges on this staff. We don't have the staff, do we?"

Kristof laughed and smacked Lionel's back. "I'm going to like you, boy!" As Petros and Walter looked at Lionel with appreciation in their eyes, Kristof explained. "The Blue Sun Staff is kept in the gold dragon's lair. We need to go and get it from Oranstakar. Normally, we'd just ask, based on the ancient treaties between the High Kings of Taysor with the All Father, but Golcir wants us to take it and leave a note explaining our intent. If Oranstakar is there, we'll ask permission but Golcir was clear on this – we do not have time to be proper." The Right Fist met their eyes one at a time and said, "We have to get the staff. Clearly." Kristof held out a letter sealed with Golcir's symbol. "This letter explains to the dragon that we are borrowing the staff and, Cuthbert willing, will return it before the Gold Dragon notices. If Oranstakar the Gold does notice, this letter assures compensation."

Petros scowled. "This feels like stealing. Why wouldn't a gold dragon just give us what we need to serve a worthy cause?"

Kristof began to answer but Hana had already shifted the illusion to depict the dragon's lair. Piled with treasure and Hana's illusionary map changed to show Oranstakar's mountain to their southwest. "And gold dragons do not like to part with their treasure. They also have a different understanding of Worth Causes and Good than the God Saint's."

* * *

Lionel pulled his cloak tightly across his face. The wind howling along the ridge they had just crossed nearly knocked him over. Though Taysor had warm days during winter, higher up in the mountains, it was still snow and ice. Amber leaves left over from autumn and frosted with ice crystals crunched under his feet. His horse, impatient to get out of the wind, nudged him forward. "Okay, okay," Lionel joked to his war horse. It made him feel better that the others were struggling like he was. Remembering how the Pragmatists had used wind magic to keep everyone comfortable last week, Lionel thought about asking Lady Hana how Cuthberic mages were different from the other Orders. *Magic for convenience clearly being one of those differences*, he noted ruefully.

Lionel had not yet traveled with veterans like these. It reassured him to see that they too struggled with maintaining a righteous demeanor in all things throughout the day. By evening meal, they talked by the campfire about the day and then recalled their failures in thought and action. It surprised Lionel to hear Kristof admit some of his. Though they had teleported from Taysor to Oranstakar's mountain, they were on the lower slopes. It would be a one-day ascent from there to the dragon's lair. Looking at the sun, Lionel guessed that they would be marching well into the night.

Kristof said, "Maybe it's my age, but I keep thinking how annoying it is this trail won't follow a straight course. The wind is too windy. The rocks are too rocky. And, Petros, you're snoring while you walk! It's keeping me awake." Kristof threw a biscuit at the Under Captain. "You think I don't envy your ability to march and sleep at the same time? Naw, but I'm sure I have other wrongs than envy and a grouchy disposition, but I want to apologize to all things under the Sun for wishing they were other than they are. May Cuthbert increase my holiness."

"May Cuthbert increase our holiness," they all said.

Taking heart from Kristof's admission, Lionel expressed his own feelings about magic. "I do not understand the need for magic. After all, we have the God Saint with us always. His angels buoy us up so that we continually draw closer toour holy goals. Yet, at each blast of wind, even my horse wishes that Lady Hana would use magic to calm the wind, or at least place it behind us and speed our ascent. I apologize to all things under the Sun, and to you Lady Hana for including you in my sin. May Cuthbert increase my holiness!"

It surprised Lionel that so many of the others' sins centered on age-related complaints. Even Lady Hana admitted to it. "Before joining the Holy Order, I would have used magic to fly us up this mountain. We'd be there already, within hours actually of our teleport. In spite of heavy combat training, I find this 'one foot in front of the other' trudge boring. My feet hurt. Not being able to fly, not using magic to massage my feet, or ease the trek..."

Lionel perked up. "Magic can do these things?" He immediately felt dumb for asking it and tried to mask his outburst. It made the others laugh.

Hana shook her head. "Oh dear, yes! It can do so much. But, 'suffering the natural,' as our Tanian neighbors would say, strengthens the body and the spirit. If our enemies do it, so must we if we are to be stronger." With a wry look in her eyes, Hana glanced at Kristof and added, "Now if the Right Fist were to order us to our destination with *all due haste*, things might be different. Combat orders being what they are, I need that order to speed up our trip."

Kristof looked up to see all eyes on him. He wilted like a flower without water under a hot summer sun. "We cannot. Golcir gave me orders about going up on foot. Oranstakar does not take kindly to magical approach by anyone. So it has always been this way I assume. Though, I take issue with your description of the Tanians as neighbors. They are enemies."

Hana bowed her head to him and said, "Their empire is, and the dragons are. But, I studied magic with them. Like Taysor, they are of all types."

Kristof nodded thoughtfully and replied, "All types of evil, some good few in their midst. But, enemies nonetheless in their slavish kowtowing to Tiamat. Maybe your training softened you, my lady." The Right Fist looked around the group and said, "Back to Golcir's orders, he believes Oranstakar has defenses that will cause us problems if we use too much magic. In fact," he said, pointing to Lionel, "one of the reasons for Lionel to be here, besides his valorous faith, is that he is too new to his divine powers to activate some of the defenses we must overcome in this quest, both here and maybe later against the three vampires."

Kristof sighed and twisted at his hips, wincing as his back popped in several places. "Sometimes, it is very hard to walk this path. I have suppressed this sin for too long. Lionel, my boy, I apologize to you under the Sun for not sharing this with you sooner. Your role is critically important. You are our newest member. It can only be you. Please do not think this some judgement about inexperience or unworthiness." Kristof pointed around the group. "Before this plays out, you will see - I prophesy it - that Lionel's value is not just his newness." He looked back to Lionel and added, "It's that insight you bring, by which you knew we did not yet have the staff. You're going to save us all, Lionel."

Not wanting to let this uncomfortable moment drag out any more, Lionel interjected, "You said orders about going up, Right Fist. What about when we leave?"

Kristof began to laugh and whacked Lionel on the back several times. "*With all due haste*, of course! The mystical lady will swoosh us down the mountain and we'll teleport back to The Temples."

* * *

Oranstakar's lair met Lionel's expectations exactly. Upon nearing the entrance, a faint smell of dust, and maybe old leather, met his nose. The air in the cavern felt dry with a sense of ageless and ancient weight. The motes glittered golden in the sunlight streaming down the shaft beside the mountain entrance.

Before them, the tunnel widened until they entered a great chamber. Overhead, stalactites reached down. A few massive ones formed into grand towers. Into these, small alcoves had been carved. Most contained books and scrolls stacked to the ceiling which, at Lionel's best guess, must be at least three hundred paces to its tallest point. Crystals along the cavern surface and within the towers caught the light of the sun shining into the cavern and made the entire area glow with a gentle warmth.

Lady Hana called out, "Great Sage! Oranstakar! The Order of Cuthbert is here. It is I, Hana of Cuthel. Right Fist Kristof is here as well." Her voice resounded throughout and came back to her as patchworks of echoes and ricochet syllables. After a few seconds, when the noise had calmed, Hana called out again, "Hello?" *HELLO... Hello... hello... lo...* echoed back.

Kristof said, "The Sage must have gone to Bloodstone with the High King. This is what Golcir thought would happen. You all know what the staff looks like. Let's find it. No one touch anything. Now, spread out. This place will not bother those of righteous intent. Stay focused."

Lionel began by picking a direction towards the back and walking there slowly. So many tomes and strange devices filled this cavern. A small silver spider caught his eye and began to sway side to side at his attention. He wanted to touch it, but shook his head. Spiders, by their very nature, were evil. Under all of Heaven, not a single spider served in the Pantheon. He repented and continued his search.

Eventually, he reached the back wall and sat down. Meditating on the staff, he prayed for assistance. A tickle in his nose told him he would be sneezing soon. Though he tried to resist, he could not. The echoes of his sneeze startled the others who called back to him. "I'm okay!" he answered. Wiping his face, he tasted salt. The salt was strong and he drew his sword, summoning its light. The back wall was salt. He had thought the milky luster of the columns and walls was simple quartz, but it was a pseudomorph replacement by salt.

When he sheathed his sword, the wall behind one of the salt columns glowed blue. "Well, we are looking for a blue sapphire staff," he mused. He walked over to investigate as the blue glow diminished. When only backlighting from the rest of his party illuminated his area, he felt forward with his hands. The wall he expected to touch was not there and he stumbled forward. "Hey!" He called back. "There's a secret passage back here. It looks like a wall, but it's just a trick." Lionel wondered if the disappointment in his voice carried through all the echoes. Being in his first dragon's lair, he realized he wanted the secret passage to be guarded, magicked, or something special. It occurred to him that perhaps the absence of magic like that was part of whatever enchantments kept this place secure.

"By Cuthbert," Petros exclaimed when he arrived. "If you were not standing in the entrance, I would not think it a tunnel at all!"

The passage led them back into another salt cavern. The air felt so dry it made Lionel's mouth crave the taste of water. Unconsciously, he grabbed a canteen from his waist and took a sip. Laid out before them in a grid, corridors masked by the same optical illusion branched at right angles. They walked straight, only pausing when Lady Hana thought she saw something of interest.

On close inspection, they noticed objects embedded in the salt. Some of the blocks contained what appeared to be books, armor, weapons, and other types of gear. Hana prayed quietly and with the last utterance falling from her lips, the items trapped in salt all around them flared to brilliant light. "These objects are all very much enchanted," Hana said pressing her hand against the crystal between her and a scepter. She closed her eyes and appeared to focus on her hand against the salt. "I'm very sure if we try to take any, bad things will happen to us."

Kristof snorted. "Our righteous hearts will overcome any traps. Surely, the Sage safeguards these against common thieves and Tanians."

Hana tapped the salt under her hand. "It's solid. It's perfect. Though this is a salt mine, these structures were created with powerful magic. I would not wish to test Oranstakar's access conditions against our righteousness. Dragons do not think the way we do."

Under Captain Petros drew his blade half way and said, "Stand back, my lady. If you wish to test with that scepter, I will gladly..." But, Hana caught his hand. "What?" he began to ask but she shushed him.

"Your movement to draw a weapon, or perhaps your intent to force the scepter changed something. Quiet," she pleaded.

With so many enchanted items blazing with colored light, Lionel noticed what appeared to be snow falling. He held out his hand and felt it. "It's salt. It's raining salt."

As Petros let go of his blade, the salt stopped falling. A growing sense of pressure faded as well. Kristof frowned at the scepter. Adorned with Pha Rannic emblems, it must be holy. "Why would the Sage trap a holy item from holy servants? We all serve the same Pha Rann."

Hana cautioned him. "Dragon, not a Sage, though he is that. Dragons, as I noted, do not see things the way we do! At least we now know what will happen when we take the Blue Sun Staff. We need to find it. That – whatever it was – was most likely a teaser." She rubbed her hand on the column again. "Did you know that salt can become molten? My guess is that the trap here is fire, of an alchemical kind we may not be able to endure."

They spread out and again Lionel found himself isolated from the others. Confident they could find each other by sound, Lionel tried to let the God Saint guide him to the staff. After a series of turns, he found himself in an open space where the ground sloped down to form a shallow bowl. In the center of the bowl, a single crystal column rose up. Lionel began walking towards it when his left boot splashed.

He bent down to look and saw a clear liquid, so clear as to be invisible, filling the depression. A sudden tingling in his foot made him look down. The liquid had rusted through his steel boots and was climbing up his greaves. With haste, he undid his leg armor, but where his fingers touched the rust, the metal in his gauntlets began to rust as well. It took too long, five minutes he guessed, to remove affected gear. When finished, only his breastplate, sword, and shield had survived. "Brothers?" he called out. "Lady Hana? I've found something."

Perfect silence answered him and he felt a building pressure. Apparently, touching the liquid had activated another magical trap. He prayed for his team to find him, confident they would. The God Saint never left his knights alone. "Together, we are mighty," Lionel whispered. Feeling he was running out of time, Lionel removed all of his metal gear. Feeling he must also shed his clothing, he did so while praying the Lady did not arrive first.

Nude, Lionel waded into the liquid. It felt soft, like warm water, but soft. A blister along one of his toes began to erupt in agony though. He tried to ignore it, but soon, the blister began to bleed. His blood leached into the perfect liquid and left a trail of his steps to the crystal column. The agony made him sweat and something about sweating made his skin react to the liquid in a most excruciating manner. Not sure he could endure the pain, Lionel drove forward to the center.

A plaque inscribed at the column's base read: *Ask your need.*

How can a blister hurt this much?, Lionel wondered. His legs, thankfully the liquid was only knee deep, were beginning to burn the same way the blister had. "Bright and Holy Lord Cuthbert, hear me," Lionel said reverently. "I ask for the Blue Sun Staff."

Nothing happened. He put his hand on the inscription and said it again. His words felt heavier this time and then searing pain, as if he were being burned by fire, made him nearly fall into the liquid. He now stood in a pool of pink blood where his immersed skin must have dissolved. His legs, in this liquid agony, were gone; he felt only excruciating fire burning below his knees. A drop of sweat fell from his nose and hissed where it hit the water. "Please, I need this. The Jade God is rampaging and we have a chance to defeat an Abyssal Power. Please, Bright Pha Rann and God Saint Cuthbert, hear me. Grant me the Blue Sun Staff."

From behind him, Lady Hana said, "You're very foolhardy to do this alone. I heard your call. Try again but this time, ask in Merakoran." Nothing. "Try Draconian," she suggested. "Here, repeat after me exactly."

This time, the crystal flared brilliant blue and shrank until the staff, exactly as Hana had depicted it, lay under his hand. It was much bigger than he had thought it would be. Picking it up from the crystal pedestal, Lionel guessed, "This must weigh fifty pounds, my lady." He labored to not let his pain affect his courtly manner.

He tried to turn and walk but pain in his bones made him cry out in agony and nearly lose his balance. Looking over his shoulder at Lady Hana, Lionel said, "Apologies for my undressed state. I was inspired but cannot move my legs. I will throw the staff over. Do not enter this accursed pool."

Lionel twisted and heaved the staff with all his might. His legs below the knee had desiccated, bled, and begun to crystalize. The twisting motion amputated his legs and Lionel fell face first into the liquid. Lionel saw the Lady Hana reach for the staff as Kristof and the others ran forward to help her catch it.

I'm going to die here… he thought. The liquid took his eyes. He felt his eyelids burn like parchment to a flame.

* * *

Lionel's senses did not want to wake up. He felt cloudy and everything was dark. His hands and legs would not move and pain radiated from any attempt to move any part of his body. *My eyes…*, he could sense only an absence of where his eyes had been. With his heart racing, Lionel tried to move, to call out for help. Nothing in his body worked and only pain answered him. He realized his hearing had turned everything into muffled thuds and only his heart, only his struggling movement brought any sound. He tried to call out for help, but felt cotton bandages in his mouth. His tongue was gone and he blacked out on the fast tread of his thudding heart and panic.

"He's very young," Hana said to Kristof. "He'll pull through. Golcir was wise to choose him. He's perfect for our mission. It takes a certain naiveté to struggle through so much pain towards the Light. Lionel has a heroic spirit."

Kristof laid his hands on Lionel's head and prayed for him to sleep. "To think that salt water could melt a body. I had my doubts about him, but he remained focused on our cause. He found it by faith where we stumbled about like fools. The God Saint chastises me to be more like Lionel." Kristof sat down opposite Hana and pulled the bandages back on Lionel's hands. New fingernails were just beginning to bud in pink skin. "Waiting is a sore trial. It makes me appreciate the other Temples and their much faster approach to healing. I considered activating the traps so that we could use Combat Orders to resurrect Lionel more quickly."

"Wisdom," Hana interrupted him. "It was wisdom, Kristof. Had you done this, who knows what may have happened? You can be sure Oranstakar would have considered a pawn sacrifice to get the staff and set countermeasures to any magic. Remember how my basic attempt to detect magic affected the caverns?"

"Blessed wisdom from Lord Cuthbert then," Kristof huffed. "I've seen a lot of damage to a human body, but never something like this. He sleeps now, but will his mind be okay? I cannot imagine."

Hana kissed Lionel's head. "He is a hero. He will pull through. I've read about Morbatten's earliest days, when some of the priestesses refused to revive fallen soldiers. They considered it a form of torture, and refused Dar Tania's orders. They were heretics. Yet, we are not so different from that them, at that time."

"Careful, sister. We are very different."

It took two more days for Lionel to awaken. He could feel active blessings throughout his entire body. Other divine powers cradled his thoughts and uplifted his spirit. Lady Hana's supple fingers unwrapped the bandages around his hands. She said, "You've had a rough go of it, young hero. Cuthbert blesses you for your sacrifice. We have the Blue Sun Staff because of you, Lionel. Be blessed."

The other three Cuthberics chimed in, "Be blessed." Lionel recognized Petros, Walter, and Kristof by their voices. They are here with me, he realized. The quest is still on. He felt excited and relieved they had not moved on without him.

Gently, she said, "You should be able to speak. Tell me your full name and rank."

Lionel tested the memory of coming to, wounded, and of not having a tongue. It felt far away from right now. His tongue felt better than fine. He realized he was starving. "I am Lionel van Farville. Rank of Knight in the Bright God's Army and servant paladin of Cuthbert, the God Saint. I'm also very hungry." He smiled as he said this and began to unwind the bandages around his eyes.

Kristof took the bandage from him and carefully unwrapped Lionel's eyes. "You gave us quite the scare, Lionel." Lionel noted the gentle touch and lack of a term like 'boy' or comments about his youth. "We have food ready for you," the old priest said. "But, take it easy. I've seen many a resurrection, but none quite like yours."

Though they treated him with tender care, Lionel felt full of energy. After a few bites and awkward questions Lionel could not answer about whether he had met the God Saint in death, they reviewed the next step in the plan with him.

Kristof leaned forward, clearly excited to tell Lionel everything. "So, we left the Sage's lair with the staff and what was left of your body and armor. Our gracious lady teleported us back to The Temples. We've been using the Blue Sun Staff to watch Bloodstone. The war there, it's beyond description and unlike any record we have in our histories! Just last night, a demi-lich attacked the Temple of Tiamat. From what we could tell, the foul creature almost killed Dar Ana. Can you believe it? We later learned that King Rojo and Legion Commander Verit died in that same fight, probably saving their lover priestess. Golcir and Vel Pajor are working the other part of this plan. Everything is moving just like Golcir predicted it would. Given the demi-lich's attack, it seems likely that any day, the Jade God will appear."

Lionel wiped his face clean from eating and asked, "Have we found Crea?"

Everyone nodded, smiles splitting their faces. Hana said, "You'd think that it'd be hard, but when all of the evil in Tania moves to Bloodstone, what's left behind is easy to see. They're in the Temple at Morbatten, near what they call the Temple Gate. So far, Tania has been moving troops to Bloodstone via that and the Eastern Plateau Gate on Dragon Mountain. We were surprised they were not in Alerius' hidden lair somewhere. To breach that with the Blue Sun Staff and to resurrect Crea would have made this epic mission into something to echo into the ages to come."

"The righteous path is strait but it is easy with faith," Petros said with a smile. "Easy as eating a biscuit."

Walter laughed and threw a biscuit to Petros. "As easy as the God Saint wishes it to be. Crea is coming home."

The light in the room, the shared mirth, the smiling laughter made Lionel feel elated. His heart sang out that it would be easy, but a small part of his brain reminded him: *You're twenty years old. You just died getting a staff. The only purpose of the staff was to find Crea. Without it, the millennial vampire would be where exactly? Even knowing he's in Tiamat's Temple does not make it easy*, and Lionel had to push that sinful and doubting voice aside. Thoughts like this were better suited to the Pragmatists. Cuthbert required absolute faith and total victory.

Lionel and the team checked and re-checked their preparations. During his recovery, they had acquired new armor for him. It put his old armor to shame and he wondered if it meant he had earned a promotion. His sword also bore the symbols of a flameblade even though he had not yet earned the right to even try for a holy sword like the veteran paladins could wield. Looking around, Lionel noted that all of them had different armor. When he squinted to read the tiny script, he was surprised to find he could not.

Petros pulled his cuirass on and whacked his chest. "It's Merakoran script, Lionel. The wizard said we would need this for added protection against the vampires, just in case. I was expecting a full argument from the Right Fist, but he just signed off on the requisition papers." Petros ran his fingers along the script, which even a few paces away looked like gold worked into the armor's creases as part of the design.

Lionel hefted his breastplate up and let it slip over his shoulders. "I know Merakor is special, but the language amplifies magic or something?"

Petros smirked and said, "I've heard lots of wizards use Merakoran script, even the dragonlovers, for defensive magic against evil. Something about how, at that time, things were closer to Heaven. It never made sense to me that a language would matter all that much. The intent and the words and action seem like the only things that would."

Lionel agreed but caught his reflection in the flameblade. They had to be ready when the time came. "Am I ready for this?" Lionel wondered out loud.

Petros came over and looked. "It's a good strong sword. Mine was just like this. Each Righteous Feat is inscribed on the blade. Someday, Lionel. Someday."

The time came while they prayed in the Temple. An image of victory filled their minds even as the hulking form of a titanic ram-headed demon broke the valley floor of Bloodstone. The God Saint showed them Orcus' arrival. They also heard a voice speak to them and, instinctively, they knew where to teleport into Tania. It was on the backside of the Temple Mount where a box canyon dropped several thousand feet to ancient fortress of Perdition. Normally guarded, in this moment, Tania's eyes had all turned to, and gazed only at Bloodstone.

Lady Hana's teleportation spell materialized them on the exact spot shown to them. Overhead, the sun's bright light looked and felt wrong. It had a sick green sliver of light rimming its eastern edge. "We'd better hurry," Kristof ordered. "Hana, in the middle. Lionel up front with me. Now, we run to the Temple."

They raced. Their armor and weapons did not slow them down at all. The God Saint uplifted their feet and carried the weight of it all as if borne by angels flying around them. Lionel rejoiced when he jumped a short wall and landed on the steps of the Temple. The lightning obelisk stone rose up ahead of their position. Hana beckoned them to her side and guided them to where the obelisk turned a corner into the Temple proper.

As they moved, she scraped the Blue Sun Staff along the wall until she detected an irregularity. She raised her fist and they stopped. "Prepare yourselves for battle," she whispered.

As she began to cast a spell, Kristof prayed over them all. "May Cuthbert's Strength be your strength. May your speed by that of the Holy Angels. May Justice be your sword. May the God Saint's Light be your armor. May Crea's atonement be our shield."

Finishing the spell, Hana pressed her hand to the wall and its grey stone rippled outwards from her hand and then fell away from her to form a circular tunnel penetrating the Temple of Tiamat. The outer wall was nearly four paces thick. Her tunneling spell clipped several chambers and ended in space. No sooner did the tunnel open than the very stone of the Temple moved to heal itself. Hana called out words of magic and the stone fell quiet. Lionel thought he heard a divine voice join Hana's in quieting the earth elementals bound to the Dragon Temple.

Kristof pointed to her and said, "Lionel, help the Lady bear the weight of the staff. Swords drawn. Combat orders. We charge!"

They ran into the Temple of Tiamat. It was empty but had a heaviness about it that hurt Lionel's eyes. The dragon motifs everywhere, the gold-inscribed draconian script, the images of Tiamat and various Dar priestesses from ancient days, to Lionel's eyes told of an ancient hunger and possessiveness. They did not just want Lionel's submission, they craved his abject love. They would only be satisfied when he wanted them with his entire being. That craving for his love smacked as blasphemous. As they moved past one he recognized as a statue of Dar Tania, he said, "I'll never serve you."

Lady Hana, unused to running this fast or carrying such a heavy staff, noted, "Good, you feel it too. They aren't kidding when they say Tehra is Tiamat's throne. From their viewpoint, we're like insects interrupting a picnic. At best, we're fans and spectators."

Ahead of them, Kristof's holy symbol blazed into brilliant daylight. It pushed back the coveting shadows and revealed three vampires standing in the central chamber. Kristof skidded to a stop and presented his symbol. Behind him, the paladins and Hana joined their faith to Kristof's as he commanded the vampires. "You will kneel before the Divine Light of Pha Rann! The God Saint would have words with the High Priest Crea. Crea, come forward"

Kristof's voice trumpeted out with confidence and faith. The three vampires looked up at the bright light. Lionel knew, as he joined his faith and power to Kristof that they would yield. He could see them kneeling.

"Brothers, prepare the Gate. I will see what they want." The vampire general Crea strode forward and stopped just an arm's length away from Kristof. Darkness met Light and for a moment, the Light held. Then it bent and warped backwards until only the Cuthberics' bodies contained any light at all. "I am Crea. What would the God Saint say to me?"

Lionel looked up. It shocked him the vampires were not kneeling. That two continued their ritual and the third stood in defiance of Kristof's power did not sit with the faith of his heart. He furrowed his brow and prayed harder to Cuthbert. Kristof's voice cracked when he said, "It is time you came home, Crea. The Abyss is too dark for an angel like you. You should be flying the Heavens…"

Crea reached out and tapped Kristof in the center of his forehead. "Yes, I should. But, that is not the destiny given to me. Instead, I was torn from Pha Rann by the Jade God and made into a slave." Crea voice had a lethal edge of bitterness that made Lionel feel sorry and scared for Kristof at the same time. For a long second it seemed Crea might feed on Kristof. Maybe the Light of Cuthbert held him back. "A slave with teeth that bite. Orcus' day is come at long last and this is the message the Heavens send to me, the angel of vengeance come to end Orcus? The God Saint would say this to me: to stop?"

Kristof tried to speak but a line of blood ran from his forehead into his mouth. He gagged and shouted, "You should be an angel of Light, Crea! Join with us. Come back to us, please. In Pha Rann's holy name, come back to the light. Do not be this angel of vengeance when you can take the same thing, but for Pha Rann."

Crea turned his back to Kristof and opened his arms to the vaulted dome of the dragon temple. His eyes rose up the tall fire obelisk, which crackled with ember light. Crea hissed, "Only Tiamat has come to my aid in thousands of years. Now, what does the God Saint offer to one as dark as I, middling paladins?" He vanished and materialized between Hana and Lionel. "Do you bring me a gift to buy my acquiescence?"

For a brief second, Lionel felt Crea's eyes lock with his and curiosity flashed through the vampire's eyes. "Ah, I see," the vampire said.

Crea's cruel laughter filled the room as, from across the way, another voice called out to him. "The Gate will be open in moments. Come, Crea. It is time."

Crea eyed Hana and took her hand off the staff to kiss it. His teeth cut lines across her knuckles and he said, "The blood of your righteous recalcitrance is sweet, dear lady. I should bring you with us, to see a god die. You are not so different from Malcolm. He too began as a mage and found religion. The things we could show you."

The nearness of the vampire froze them all. The threat and the offer together pulled at them with allure but also revulsion. Lionel felt Hana tremble. Holding the simple thought that they must keep their faith focused on Kristof or die was the only thing they could do. Their bodies would not move.

Hana mustered the strength to scream "No!" and shoved Crea back from her. He did not move but the might of Hana's push threw her back from Crea and out of Kristof's light.

Lionel flinched to catch her fall. The cold feel of Crea's hand prevented Lionel from even moving. Time seemed to pause and then, as if unable to stare at anything else, Lionel watched Crea put his hand over Lionel's hand on the Blue Sun Staff. He squeezed.

Lionel screamed as his fingers broke around the staff. Lionel's eyes followed Hana and then his thoughts altered and became not his own. Crea continued to squeeze while his mind-voice thundered in Lionel's brain. "A great darkness is rising in Nientro. This staff is key to creating a counter-dominion against my brothers. Remember these words, and this…" Crea squeezed Lionel's hand so hard the staff splintered against his bones and drove broken wood and sapphire fragments into his flesh. "Remember this moment, paladin."

Crea was gone. Lionel's pain-filled eyes found Crea standing before a gaping portal of blackness. Abyssal energy blasted out from it. Lionel ignored it and pulled Hana back into Kristof's light. The high priest reached out for Crea and screamed, "An angel could go there for Heaven! Do not do this, Crea! You can serve your design and advance Heaven's too! For the right reason! Join with us!"

Crea stepped through the portal after the other two. Their woeful presence immediately let go its hold on the Cuthberics and they breathed deeply. They would not be left alone in the Temple for long. Hana tried to heal Lionel's hand but it refused to heal. Neither could they separate the staff from his broken grip. Worse, Lionel felt a compulsion in his heart. "Brothers, my lady," he said through gritted teeth. "We must follow them. Crea helps us because our cause is just. We are never alone in righteous deeds. Even if our ally is a vampire. Even if we heed evil. Test your hearts; this is what Golcir requires us to do for the God Saint, for Creation itself!"

"Sacrilege!" Petros screamed and drew his sword. "You've been corrupted in your head."

All around them, from the obelisks of the fire, ice, and lightning dragons, golems of stone wrapped about in steel runes rose up, menacing them. Hana threw herself between Lionel and Petros. "We don't have time for this. We must decide: trust Lionel or leave!"

Kristof pushed Petros' sword away from Lionel. "Check your heart, Undercaptain. The God Saint urges us to charge into the Abyss! Combat Orders; we march on the Abyss!"

Without another word, the group ran after the three vampires. With each step, Lionel heard a voice, mighty like a rushing river but with a smooth surface, and it said, "By many swords is Evil defeated. My friends, take courage and faith." Lionel looked at his arm and saw goosebumps. He had never heard Cuthbert speak to him like this, like a concerned friend. He could tell the others must have heard it too.

* * *

Lionel's eyes struggled to adjust to their new location. Overhead, a yellow-green sun blazed down with an indifferent light. His shadow on the dry dust of this place was split into two, one yellow and one green. The light had a malevolent spirit in it but seemed directed away from this place. *So this is the Endless Worlds*, Lionel thought.

The Cuthberics took it all in and Kristof dropped to his knees and begged Cuthbert for power and might to press forward. "Great God Saint, we stand in the blackest depths of evil and pray for your divine power. Lend us your strength that we might achieve the unachievable. Let the glory of our quest carry our prayer to the Heavens!"

Lionel waited for the blessing that would inevitably come. Instead, they heard a voice speaking as plain as if Walter had said it. Like before they entered the gate, it was mighty but sounded so far away it could barely be heard. "Dear friends, my brothers. My sister. You stand in the Endless Worlds of Necromancy, out of my reach. So, I make you my angels, to buoy you up and give you what I cannot. My day is come to face the Jade God, and then my rebellious brother. Lend me your faith as I make you my own right arm."

Tendrils of white light speared through by gold burst from the Cuthberics' shoulder blades. With the wings of light came strength to move in this fell place. Lionel leapt to his feet and swung the Blue Sun Staff like a club. His hand still ached but he was able to ignore it in his new uplifted state. He tried to peel his broken fingers off the staff, but could not. His sword materialized in his other hand and he roared at the green sun. The others did the same and then Kristof flew after the three vampire mages. The four followed, struggling to catch up to the high priest. They felt the angelic power in their bones and with it came something else - the desire to impress their god and prove their worth with this boon.

Ahead of them, the vampires became aware of their pursuit. Crea and Malcolm swerved to either side to come back and strike at their flanks. The center vampire, Nientro, rotated in air and began spell-casting. Holding the staff, Lionel felt knowledge dawn in his mind and he knew. "Nientro is going to cast a spell that will fill us with divine power. It will act like a magnet and draw chaos creatures to us!"

Nientro's spell filled the horizon before them with golden light. The Cuthberics rose up into the flat brown sky, easily dodging the spell with Lionel's warning. Petros did not dodge and let the Nientro's spell baptize him with holy power. He screamed, "Then I will take this power and defeat whatever evil comes at me!"

The golden light drained from the sky into Petros, filling his angel wings and countenance with unbearable beauty and light. Petros screamed into the sky and darted to attack Crea. Filled with energy from Nientro's spell, he left a trail of golden light behind him.

From Crea and Malcolm, lightning attacks crackled at them from impossibly far away. The vampires were exceedingly powerful in this place, the seat of necromancy's power. One of the bolts struck Walter, who fell like a shooting star to smash into the ground.

Lionel swerved to give aid to Walter as Nientro's next attack materialized black whips, miles long that see-sawed through the air. Though the group dodged with Lionel's warning, one of the whips slammed into Lady Hana and sent her somersaulting through the air towards Malcolm.

Crea's next attack on Kristof occurred so quickly, Lionel did not even see it until the angel wing fell, severed. Kristof flapped a few times trying to correct his attitude and then fell. Petros swerved from attacking the vampire and caught Kristof to help him land. Dropping the Right Fist into the sand, Petros whirled to re-engage.

The vampire general was right back in Petros' face. The Cuthberic, swollen with power, smashed his helmet visor into Crea's forehead and stumbled back, flapping erratically. Undaunted and seemingly unaffected by the bold attack, Crea caught hold of Petros' pinion feathers and tore them free. "Fool," he said. "Already, they come for you. If you cherish your friends, you will flee this place and lead them away from your allies."

Petros swung his sword but the vampire easily dodged the flailing blade as he spun Petros about by one wing in the air. When Crea stopped spinning abruptly, Petros' momentum rolled him into the vampire who caught Petros' head and locked his gaze against a far horizon. The crackling of broken angel wings snapped throughout the Endless Worlds. A cloud of dust had appeared there. "See? Your bright power summons chaos spawn. They hunger for the energy Nientro gave and you foolishly took. It makes you powerful, but you are still overmatched. You were never strong enough… and you fail your God Saint over and over again."

Petros struggled to break free of the grip but could not, entwined in his wings and quivering against the vampire's body. Crea pointed again. "See your doom. I'm going to let you go." A flood of healing energy spasmed through Petros' body and broken wings. Crea whispered, "If you're wise, you will run. If you attack me, I will kill you and then those will kill your allies."

Crea threw Petros back from him. Wings coming unfurled, Petros caught his fall in a moment of indecision. Far below him, Kristof had recovered on the ground, but was bleeding profusely from the amputated wing. Lionel could fight but was tending to Walter. Lady Hana was in a bad way though Petros could not see anything obviously wrong with her. Petros clenched his sword and squared his shoulders. "Crea, you were one of the greatest of the Sun!" he yelled.

Crea bowed with a flourish and a cat's grin. "I was. But, my destiny long ago departed the pathways to Heaven. Now, save your friends and run!"

Petros looked at Kristof hoping for guidance but the priest was lost in communion with Cuthbert. Or, at least, it looked like he was praying. Petros saw a horde of writhing flesh within the dust cloud as it came closer. The flesh loosely conformed to spheres. Some rolled in the dirt, while others flew or bounced. All were a tangle of misshapen limbs, eyes, and mouths, so many mouths. For, while Chaos can create, without a beautiful design, its creations tended to be monstrous, and above all else, it hungered.

Petros lifted his head to the sky and wished for a golden sun against a sapphire sky. "In righteousness, we are never alone. Good-bye, my friends." He flew at a perpendicular angle away from his comrades, the vampires, and the horde. He hoped and was glad to see the chaos spawn follow his bright path. The brown and green desert stretching into infinite space before him filled him with hope he could put enough distance between himself and his brethren. Images of an eternal battle filled his thoughts. A quieter voice, Crea's, chased him and assured him, "You're going to fight them and die, except you won't really die, stupid paladin. You will become your own enemy, forever twisting in on yourself, a parody of the angel you are now."

Petros grimly ignored the voice and committed to letting these chase him for however long it took. "Maybe they will grow bored." But, despair answered him: *Chaos is never bored. Petros, you're just a plaything to Eternal Hunger.*

Lionel found Walter. Blisters full of blood bubbled his flesh. The lightning had flash-cooked the paladin in his armor. The staff allowed Lionel to see that Walter was alive, barely. With what faith and power he had, Lionel laid his hands on Walter and prayed. By Cuthbert's power, he felt Walter's pulse strengthen and his lifeforce revive. The severity of the wounds, though, remained. Walter was so badly injured that angelic healing barely made a visible difference.

Walter caught Lionel's hand and said, "They don't see it. But, you do. They will fight to the death. I've seen Petros do this. With an angel's power, it will be to the death… Kristof and Hana too." Walter choked and began coughing. Around them, the battle raged between the vampires and the other three Cuthberics.

Lionel did not need to look to know they were overmatched. He said, "Golcir's mission was for us to resurrect Crea. Only Kristoff and Hana could even attempt that. Without Crea's cooperation, I see what you mean. There has to be another way."

Walter's eyes rolled back in his head. From the brown sky overhead, black rips opened around the green sun. The jagged tears, like lightning scarred the sky. Unlike lightning they did not fade. From the portal area they had entered with the Vampire Generals, a flash of light and a sound like the screaming of a million souls blasted the landscape.

A voice bubbled throughout the ground, radiated from the jagged sun, and declared, "The gnats sting. Why do they sting?" Lionel's thoughts flashed and he realized the Blue Sun Staff had connected him to Orcus. An image of those titanic dragons burned in his mind. He saw a dragon priestess with long black hair that burned with flames. She stood before Orcus and pointed swords at his eyes, and then the vision left Lionel's mind. "They sting. I will see... I will see them all."

As if trying to help, or to obey, the ground around them flexed and millions of eyes blinked and opened in what had been dust. Where Lionel's boots pressed into them, they popped and oozed gore. Walter quivered as the ground around his armor hardened and then became wet. "What just happened? Do I want to know?"

"No, brother. The Jade God stands in Bloodstone. A raven-haired priestess just attacked the god's eyes."

"Ana, that must be Ana. I bet she was smiling," Walter said coughing. "Is it a sin that I found her beautiful?"

Lionel's attention was caught as the staff vibrated in his arm and another vision came to him. He shook his head, "Shhh, brother. No, finding beauty is not a sin. It's part of the design. I'm sure of it." A club, maybe a mace, filled his mind. It had three sides, each a leering and seemingly aware skull of shadowed green eyes and fangs. All of the dragons, and griffins, and so many attacks moved towards Orcus that Lionel could not count them.

The Blue Sun Staff filled his mind with numbers and types of attacks. Eight fortresses, forty siege golems each, one hundred and seventy mages, three thousand and twelve clerics, ten dragons, and eighty griffons, attacking at ranges now filling his mind. Lionel knew he saw exactly fifty-eight attacks simultaneously redirect to strike the mace – no, the Sceptre of Orcus – at the exact same point just below the skull heads. Ten dragon attacks each somehow hit the same point on the mace. Wondering, another image filled his mind of black-robed mages bearing Tiamat's emblems enacting powerful magic to alter the course of reality so that this would happen, so that the mighty Wand of Orcus would break.

"The sun!" Orcus commanded and Lionel's vision turned green.

He coughed and begged, "Please, stop. I cannot. Focus, Lionel. Me. Here. Now." He looked for Hana and saw her too far away to easily reach. The staff seemed to respond to his attempt to focus on Lady Hana. Information about her state came flooding into his mind. She was considering a self-destructive magic as a last ditch attempt to delay if not hurt one of the vampires. Lionel found himself full of admiration for her fighting spirit but felt a knot of concern grow in his gut. Things had gone from bad to worse too quickly. He wondered how Golcir fared with the primary plan… and the Blue Sun Staff filled his mind with a terrible battle scene. The Supreme Commander flew with angels at full charge towards a gate of bone and bleeding skin. Besought by hellhounds on all sides, liches awaited him before that awful gate.

Against his contemplation, Cuthbert's voice came to them all again. "The portal called Bomoki's Gate is destroyed. It is time for me to enter Bloodstone. The Jade God is trapped in Tehra. Remember your mission my stalwart angels!"

Perhaps the vampires heard the voice too. Malcolm and Crea fell back to guard Nientro, who began casting another spell. Kristof and Hana huddled together. Petros had already left, seeming to abandon them. Then, with enhanced vision, Lionel saw the horde of abyssal demons giving Petros chase. The staff swelled his mind with information about the nature of the horde and he had a glimpse of Petros' sacrifice for them all. Had he not taken the energy, had that infusion hit any of them, the flood of chaos beasts would be chasing any hit.

Just two Cuthberics stood against the three vampires: Kristoff and Hana. From Walter's position hundreds of paces away, Lionel reverenced the heroic sacrifice Kristof and Hana were about to make. "They're going to die," he whispered.

Walter nodded his head. "It'll be beautiful. Lionel, Sir Lionel, you're the only one left who can act. If we cannot resurrect Crea, what else can we – can you do?"

Lionel looked down at the Blue Sun Staff. It had belonged to Crea thousands of years ago. Crea had told him to remember, to prevent the unleashing of an evil even greater than the Jade God. The staff now flooded Lionel's mind with information about Crea, how he had had a vision and secreted the staff away with gold dragons to be retained against a time of great need.

Lionel understood that if Necromancy fell, there would be a moment here in the Endless Worlds without a master. It was not just what had been explained by Kristof and Hana. It was more than that. The normal Ascension principles would not apply; anyone here in the Endless Worlds could claim Necromancy. As if shooing a gnat away, Lionel dismissed the idea that he could become the Master of Necromancy.

Even as he thought it, the Blue Sun Staff showed him information that confirmed what a foolhardy course that would be. He laughed at himself and said, "It hardly seems possible, but Crea is concerned that with the Jade God's death, an even more terrible evil will be unleashed. He said something about counter-dominion."

Overhead, the brown sky continued to crack revealing a gaping black space. It looked like a nighttime sky devoid of stars. Nientro hovered in the air before the center of the expanded fissure. He shouted, "Hear me, slaves of Orcus! Bomoki's Gate is destroyed! Your master's death draws nigh at Tiamat's hand! In this moment, you have free will. In this moment, you get to decide. If you choose to serve me, I will set you free. Show me your signets into the sky and join me. Or fall with Orcus, I care not. Necromancy shall fall!"

Lionel tried to cover his ears against the volume of Nientro's command. Seeing Walter in pain, he covered Walter's ears as best he could. In the vast silence following Nientro's challenge, Kristof charged Nientro. Hana swept after him. Divine radiance from their wings and the power of their faith and Hana's magic fired Lionel's imagination. Lionel knew, if he survived, he would never forget the perfect beauty of this moment. "I bear witness forever," he vowed. He felt Walter nod.

Amidst the darkness of the shredded sky, a single light winked into being. Then, more and more began to fill the black canvas of the broken dominion. Nientro ignored the Cuthberics' attack while Crea and Malcolm both moved to intercept. The vampire general laughed and jumped towards the crumpling sun now torn by black streaks. Nientro's body burned away into an incorporeal mass of shadows, like viscous ink thrown into the air. Lionel marveled to realize the shadows were encapsulating the sun, somehow. He dismissed the thought before the Staff might tell him more. He did not need the distraction of more knowledge.

Kristof pointed his Holy Symbol of Cuthbert at Crea and called – again - for the vampire to resurrect. The execution of the prayer was flawless. Lionel felt its purity and helped Walter sit up to watch.

Crea shrugged its effects off while a mace of evil spikes and piercing needles appeared in his hand. Malcolm summoned a sword of red energy that made Lionel feel insane whispers in his mind. The voices stopped when he looked away from the blade, but they urged him to commit suicide on Malcolm's sword.

"So much evil power," Lionel said. "I never doubted the teachings, but that Morbatten would harbor such wicked creatures..." His words went dry as fear vaporized his mouth's water. And, those terrible weapons moved forward to attack Kristof and Hana like the sun setting, like the wind blowing.

Before Malcolm's sword could strike Kristof, Nientro's ghost form of inky tendrils swirled into Kristof's body. Malcolm fell back, stopping just shy of skewering the priest. The divine radiance of the God Saint vanished. His cherished holy symbol fell. Hana called to him, trying to touch him, hoping to use their combination of powers to augment Kristof against whatever attack this might be.

Crea swung his needled mace at Hana. When it connected with her hip, her body blasted down into the brown monochrome sands. Lionel noted how broken her body seemed as it fell, and prayed for her soul. *It's barely there*, the staff answered his unformed question. *She lives still*. The mace shattered her pelvis. She was bleeding internally. Even with magical healing, she could die. It all depended on whether Crea had activated cursing magic in the mace.

Lionel could not know, could not comprehend, Nientro's attack against Kristof. The Blue Sun Staff struggled to articulate a mix of possession, soul jarring, and domination. Kristof grabbed Hana's neck to pull her back into the sky. She struggled to send her faith to Kristof. The flock of shadows around Kristof elongated into an arm that reached from the sky to the earth in a single blink. With a leering grin, Kristof began a prayer to Cuthbert, one to unwind her life: anti-resurrection.

Lionel saw it all from the Blue Sun Staff. The instant Nientro's phantom touched Kristof, the Right Fist's spirit all but vanished. It was still there, but just barely, like the vestige of white robes dragged through mud and only a few patches remain clean.

Crea's words from the Temple of Tiamat slammed into Lionel's mind: REMEMBER. It was not Kristof who casually snapped Hana's neck and tossed her body aside. It was not a Cuthberic who twisted Kristof's resurrection prayer to torture Hana. The Blue Sun Staff showed Lionel the tiny sliver of Kristof and how it might be freed. Nientro was having fun with the anti-resurrection prayer but Lionel guessed he had less than a minute to take action.

Lionel patted Walter on the shoulder. "Witness me, my brother Walter," Lionel said solemnly.

The angel wings obeyed Lionel's request to aid Kristof. Though the God Saint did not answer the raging prayer of Lionel's soul, Lionel knew his god heard him… and sped him faster. Glancing at the two vampires, Lionel noticed Malcolm move to intercept his attack. Crea, however, caught Malcolm and said something. The two stood back to watch Nientro toy with Lady Hana. With some bitterness, Lionel guessed they were not worried by the young paladin, no doubt easy entertainment to their true purpose here.

The staff showed Lionel how valiantly Kristof fought against Nientro's possession. It made his heart sing with hope even while it mourned his friends. "Your deaths are not in vain," Lionel prayed. The Blue Sun Staff swung at Nientro's mid-section and hit with the full force of Lionel's speed and angelic strength. The blow rippled the air between them and blasted Nientro up into the sky.

Lionel skid to a stop and checked on Lady Hana's condition. Like Walter, she lived, but by the barest thread. It occurred to Lionel that the vampires were intentionally not slaying them outright… and while he knew that should terrify him, his anger overwhelmed reason and he spun to face Nientro.

The vampire general in Kristof's body recovered his stance one hundred or so paces away. The ground cratered around them by the force of Lionel's strike. "Impressive attack, boy," Nientro taunted him. "We spared the female and your friend over there hoping you would witness and understand. You've lost one brother to chaos spawn. How would you like to die and be responsible for your friends' deaths too?"

Malcolm called out, "We should ignore this gnat, brother. Tania's purpose is nearly fulfilled and it won't matter. Even if this boy attacked us continually, our own purpose is so close."

Nientro bowed to Malcolm's wisdom. Hoping for tactical advantage and perhaps surprise, Lionel attacked again. The angel's wings carried him the distance in a blink. This time, Nientro tried to dodge, but Lionel used the staff to catch and throw Nientro into the sky. Though the vampire could fly with magic alone, Kristof could not. Angels are faster than flight. He soared on raptor wings of golden sunlight and he carried a world of blue light in his hands. Like a ballista bolt aimed at Nientro, Lionel battered the tumbling vampire's body away from the two other generals, towards Walter.

As Lionel gave chase, the cracked sun overhead abruptly went black. The vast realm of the Endless Worlds heaved and deflated as everywhere, Orcus' dominion, and possession of this realm, dissolved into the nether energies of the Abyss. With the last light in the sky gone, the stars pledged to Nientro now blazed all the brighter. Nientro easily dodged Lionel's ongoing attacks now, and the three vampires looked up at the sun. Nientro reached his hands up at the sun as if to hold it.

Nientro's total disdain for Lionel infuriated the paladin, who tried to retain holy focus, then gave in to the holy fury burning in his gut. The staff, though, had shown Lionel what to do. It would work, and Lionel did not care about the consequences. Crea was right; they had to prevent another evil from subverting Necromancy.

"You cannot even defeat a novice paladin!" Lionel screamed. His attack battered Kristof's body into the sky again. The angel then slammed the body back and forth, keeping it airborne and praying the other two vampires would not interfere; they did not. Even Nientro was focused on the sun. Though the possessed body showed bleeding, wounds, and damage, Nientro kept the eyes focused on where the sun had been. After five consecutive blows, Nientro's eyes flared with unnatural light and he dropped Kristof's body to the ground. The staff breezed through the incorporeal mist of Nientro's body. Kristof's body fell.

This is the moment, Lionel prayed. *God Saint, please let Cuthbert catch and save Kristof. For I cannot.* The heartfelt and unspoken prayer occurred at the same moment that Lionel brought the angel sword in his right hand down onto the staff, where Crea had fractured it under Lionel's palm.

He sensed, in the moment before connecting, Nientro's disdain for yet another novice attack. The smirk of conceit that someone so young and stupid would so utterly miss his target with an enchanted blade… and then Nientro's eyes widened and he at last recognized the Blue Sun Staff.

Crea's voice slammed into Lionel's mind: I WILL REMEMBER YOU, NOBLE PALADIN OF CUTHBERT. I HONOR YOU. There was a flash of light at the staff's breaking point.

Walter's wings dragged him forward to catch Kristof's body on his back and then he rolled as the sky above them filled with roiling blue waves of plasma energy. In the flash, the stars overhead became unhidden to show thousands of hellhounds watching the events with evil fascination.

Malcolm's voice shouted out warning, "Nientro!"

Against that call, Crea answered, "Nientro has ascended, not as the God of Necromancy, but as the God of Possession. It suffices for this realm, let Necromancy be unshackled. Perhaps you and I shall claim it for Nientro."

The azure fire, like water contained in a glass bowl, twisted and writhed as serpents made of lightning. In the center, Nientro tried to pull his body together but it kept breaking apart. From it, like a comet, fell Lionel's body. Walter lifted his head through the dust of the explosion and saw. "I witness thee, Sir Lionel."

Walter saw the Lady Hana waiting for her own death an impossible distance away. He could make it if the vampires left him alone. He struggled to his feet and then pulled Kristof up over his shoulders. With a wary eye on Crea and Malcolm, Walter limped to Lady Hana. When he stumbled, his broken wings slammed into the ground to hold him upright. He knew, without looking, that Nientro wanted to kill him, wanted him more than dead. Yet, each time that horrible desire reached him, the seething blue light would pull Nientro's form apart.

Walter moved from foot to step to broken wing and counted each. That he was not attacked, that he was allowed to move, humiliated him. "Too weak for them to bother me," he muttered to himself. "One hundred… four hundred… one thousand steps…" and it kept going on. When Walter at last dropped Kristof and himself at Hana's side, he had lost count. Kristof's right gauntlet held the tokens of recall that a Cuthberic would only ever use when the lives of his fellows were at stake. "I wish I could take you with us, Sir Lionel, Under Captain Petros." He touched the recall token to Lady Hana's heart and whispered, "Fly home." Her body vanished. He sent Kristof next. The struggle to reach Hana had reopened the burn wounds across his body.

There were tokens for each of them. Petros and Lionel would not need theirs. Leaving them behind would create a risk to The Temples. Walter touched the tokens to the sand and sent them home. Walter cradled the last token to his heart and looked around. "So, this is the Endless Worlds. Good-bye, Sir Lionel. May the angels guard you eternal battles. Fly home."

* * *

Walter appeared in the Temple of the God Saint to be greeted by a Pragmatist cleric wearing Tanian armor. The Temple was just as empty as they had left it days ago. The cleric had pulled Hana and Kristof off the holy circle where recall tokens brought their users. Walter felt his angel wings leave as the Temple's Circle became real around him. His body smoldered and pus from burn blisters wept liquid around his body. He dropped to his knees and then fell face forward. "Save them," he pled.

"You already did, Son of Cuthbert," the Pragmatist answered.

Walter choked. "Sir Lionel...?"

The Pragmatist shook his head no.

* * *

Lionel choked on sand and coughed. His angel wings were gone. He felt nauseated. His eyes barely functioned and he thanked the God Saint for the small blessing of awareness. He coughed again and felt his ribs moving unnaturally in his rib cage. A movement rustled the sand past his head. He tried to call out, but spasms wracked his lungs.

A mind voice spoke to him. "That was a noble sacrifice. It ranks with the greatest heroes of Merakor. I removed you from the desolation of Nientro. A new counter-dominion is opening. It calls to me, but I have not yet decided to take it as my own."

"C-Crayuh. You, why?"

The mental connection seemed amused. "Like the sun setting, the coming of darkness is natural. You fear it, but I have been forced to make it my home. I am beyond redemption and have come to terms with it. It is better to be lord of the hell I make than to serve in another's. I am content with my path. I know you do not understand. Pha Rann would not welcome me to Heaven, nor I it."

Lionel fought upright. He had cut through his hand into the staff. The resulting explosion had cauterized his lost hand diagonally across his knuckles. His thumb remained, for now. He looked in fascination at the stumps where he imagined he could feel his fingers clenching into a fist. He coughed and said spasmodically, "You, you, you could have stopped this at any time." It took Lionel an embarrassingly long time to speak these words.

Crea did not interrupt him or use the mind link to finish or answer. "No, I could not have stopped any of this. My moral agency was stripped from me by Orcus long ago. I was lost to a darkness I could not help but love, serve, and take joy in. Nientro came to me in that darkness. Our rebellion took a very long time to yield freedom, and revenge is at last mine. To betray Nientro now would strip me of the one choice I made and owned through all the darkness of my enslavement to Orcus. I have no regrets. I have no wish to betray my only friend. You serve Cuthbert and strive to rejoice in the great deeds of heroic paladins in epic feats. You cannot imagine what is like to be compelled to rejoice for all time. Nientro is becoming a new god, the likes of which has not yet existed."

"This is Ascension?" Lionel asked.

Crea nodded. "Ascension to immortality is a series of rites. The first is the easiest. It's a confrontation with your own belief system. Most immortals-to-be confront and pledge service to that. This is how some gods end up with a pantheon. If, however, you forsake that, you have to confront each variation of your own belief system. Think of it as a test of your will. Pha Rann determined from the start that any sentient creature could ascend, but if they could not hold their focus through the vast time of the universe, they would fail as a god and be too destructive to the perfect design." Crea pointed to Nientro. "That's what he did. You and the others were his last test. A challenge of the polar opposite.

He really should have recognized it. Malcom pointed it out to him." A smile crept into Crea's voice. "Of course, I noted that you were all so weak, it did not matter. Had Nientro defeated you right from the start, his Ascension would be complete. Instead, your interruption has added something interesting into the new dominion: a spice. Though, it might be better to say it is a blind spot. This new thing will become increasingly blind to the kind of faith you brought here, Lionel. Well done."

Lionel was feeling better and realized Crea was lending him strength, was healing him. The Cuthberic in him cringed away from that dark power, but the welcome relief it brought was too much for him to not be grateful. "Thank you," he said, rubbing dead skin from his eyelids. His hair had burned away. "I do not know what a counter-dominion is."

Crea helped Lionel stand up. The desert stretched forever in all directions. The green sun now burned blue and from it a shrieking cry of hate rang out through the world. "That is Nientro. Think of it like a cocoon. Eventually, he will break free of this, his last ascension rite. He will take "possession" as his dominion, though "soul transference" would be a more accurate way of describing it. That enables a counter-dominion. Tell me, Sir Paladin, what would counter possession?"

Lionel stretched and felt his body renewing. "It would have to ownership of one's body, or something like that."

Crea nodded and spoke with words now. "Yes, something like that. Consider it: soul anchoring. Mages already know how to bind souls, but a soul trapped in a gem is just a trapped soul. What if you could anchor it in a gem? Would the gem become sentient or would the soul become crystal?" Crea pointed to the bright stars blazing visibly even with the blue sun. "Who should control such a dominion? Would it be another vampire general? My brother Malcolm seeks to claim vampirism from the Warp Lord Asmodei. He may succeed. He is strong. For me, I am considering a different way. It is not fit for someone as black as I to control the counter-dominion to what might be the darkest of all arts: total violation of the individual."

Lionel watched Nientro's body struggling to form in the blue energy. "It belongs to Heaven," he said simply.

Crea reached up to the black sun and eyed it through the gray skin of his fingers. "Yes, it does. To someone bright, straightforward, wise, focused on what might be, and who has knowledge of Nientro and what has happened here. I suppose a certain mix of youthful vigor and naïve trust would not hurt either."

Lionel turned to face Crea and said, "You would be perfect! Lord Crea, come with me. Resurrect. Repent. Take this dominion for Heaven! I will explain all that you did for us…"

"Does the ocean notice a rain drop?" Crea's rhetorical question felt like a face slap to Lionel. "Does a dragon notice a mosquito? What you say is compelling but impossible. You do not know how far I have fallen, how far I have gone to attain vengeance, to ensure no others fall prey to Orcus."

"But you…"

Crea poked Lionel in the chest. "No, you. You, Sir Lionel. This counter-dominion must belong to someone not yet corrupted by power and its trappings. I consider this my last defiance of Pha Rann, Orcus, Nientro-who-will-be, and my own dark self. Against Pha Rann's 'beautiful design,' how far I have fallen. It aches and I spit this pain back into the eye of god."

Crea grabbed Lionel's head in his hands and touched their foreheads together. "Ascend, Lionel van Farville of Cuthbert. Take the counter-dominion of soul anchoring. Give it to your bright God Saint. I know it will be jealously guarded for all of Heaven in the God Saint's hands. Remember, this is the only salvation against Nientro's power… and it will be terrible. Trust me, I know what I am talking about."

Lionel felt himself falling, towards Heaven.

ERIC K. BARNUM

CREATION

EVERYDAY ANGELS

Everday Angels

The Temple of Angels' amphitheater was barely a fifth full. I had to resist a grumpy sigh when I reimagined it full of eager students, as it had been I was younger. The worst part of it, for me at least, was that lectures about honor and the scenarios that challenge it were far more engaging than rhetorical discussions about angels. In the faith of Imperius, angels are a given. The public, in general, came because they wanted to see the Temple of Angels, or rest here after visiting The Temples, and there were many to the Gods of Creation. Sure, I had a few students required to listen because their masters ordered it. Some of the public, obvious by their attire, came because they hoped for a visitation by an angel; it had been known to happen. Most came because they knew the Temple of Angels was cool in the summer, had good food for free, and my lecture hall held a commanding view of Taysor. The great city sprawled out behind me.

I regather my thoughts and continue with my millionth disposition on this topic. "The difference between acting like an angel, being with angels, and actually being an angel is of course, whether or not angels are real." I point to the slate board where my crude drawing attempts to illustrate this. The class before me looks glazed and bored. I rub the bridge of my nose and long for my lost days of youth. I slam my hand on the table. "Look. I know. You all came here thinking you'd see an angel. Whether you see one or not, you all know they are real. How do we know this?"

Several hands go up. I'm not surprised. The few paying attention are all paladins. This topic bores even the clerics. The god Imperius is known to visit his clerics with angels only rarely. Paladins though… there's a joke: *How many paladins does it take to fight a behemoth? Just one – the angels do all the fighting.* That same joke for clerics? *The behemoth wins.*

One of the paladins is middle-aged woman. She has been intent and unwavering in her studies, even here in my Philosophies of the Divine class. We all know she is a late-blooming prodigy. Imperius himself must have touched her. "Lady Ceanne, how do we know?"

She stands up and squares her shoulders. I appreciate the sound of her joints crackling and pray to the gods to restore her youth. "We know because angels fought with us against the Jade God. The Temple of Angels is dedicated to each visitation. There are hundreds documented as statues and artwork here. We also know because some few of us are blessed to see them." Her eyes gleam into mine and I know that she sees and knows. "They walk among us, Master Yussef. I have seen them."

Some of the peasants and lower class attendees look at her with awe. She looks like she might have come from their ranks. Ceanne's face shows pox scarring not healed by a cleric. Her hair and demeanor, even after a year with us, still kowtows to nobility. They sense it. It's beyond annoying to me that the courtiers and noblemen here on holiday do as well. You can draw a line between those impressed by her faith and those who distrust her as a liar. I'm about to put them all in their place.

A priest, barely half her age, suppresses a yawn. "What good are angels if they walk among us? We only need them when a miracle is required beyond what Imperius grants our faith."

I feel a flash of righteous anger. It steels my tendons and fires my blood. "Your attitude brings dishonor to the Temple. Maybe you would be better suited for a Pha Rannic Order, Young Ian," I say gently but with a chilly tone. "Imperius requires an understanding that divine power flows to us from angels. When you heal a wound or cast out a disease, your hands are but an instrument. They are wielded…"

"By angels," Lady Ceanne finishes. "Even healers." She looks at the bored priest and smirks. "Even healers are just tools. You remind me of a blunt chisel."

The priest looks at her and, seeing the challenge in her eyes, blushes and squirms down into his seat. He looks at me, but I'm ready to fight him too. Our religion does not much care for nobility and the arbitrary drawing of social structures. Well, I concede, we care about patrons, I guess.

Ian's cowing complete, I flash a wicked smile and say, "Best not let the angels hear you say such things, any of you. Best not. For they listen. They are here with us, even if we don't see them. And, Ian, they see you. Honor fuels their willingness to empower your prayers. But," I wag my finger. "Don't worry. I'm going to send a note to your master with some required reading. I think the Soliloquies of Honorable Grand Master Chozu will be appropriate." I wait for it to sink in. Ian does not know how long these are. I sigh, audibly this time. The new priests are so,… *new.* "Now, who can tell me why angels are dismissed as the miracles they are?"

Lady Ceanne knows the answer and remains standing. When no one else speaks up, she declares, "Because the people are so out of touch with the divine, they do not even recognize them as angels. There could be an angel standing in the room with us right now, like yours Master Yuusef, and most here would notice."

I segue from her spot-on answer to several ancient accounts of times when angels fought alongside us, entire armies of angels. My class is looking at me more intently, some are praying. I wonder if my angel will show herself to any of them. A small child held in her mother's arms breaks into a grin and reaches out to Jun. I declare, "In times of war, the faithful could see them and our enemies could not, except as flashes of brilliance in tactics and luck in dodging sure attacks. In popular retelling of a Bloodstone campaign, a hellhound's bite was held back from an unconscious young paladin. Let me tell you about this and some of the other times. A hellhound is a mighty foe and even Tanians reported seeing the angel fight the hound." A few students perk up when I mention ancestors bearing their namesakes.

Alas, public knowledge of the Temple of Angels is now dwarfed by popular fascination with Khasran martial arts. According to popular legend – a legend I know to be fact - these martial arts stem from close observation of paladins long ago fighting in perfect unison with their angel. It occurred to a high priest, many millennia ago in lost Merakor, that one could study and document the movements. They started as prayers, until the ancient master noticed that all angels fought with the same movements. Testing them out against actual opponents led to a new style of unarmed combat. We call them kinetic prayers, but the Imperics to our south called them by a different name: wushu.

What is now the Khasran branch of Imperics came from ancient families that openly embraced this style of unarmed combat and made it part of their worship, part of their progression in the Temple of Angels. I could not deny that the angels loved it. My own angel always felt tranquil, calmer when I went through the motions. Hand, fist, turn, lift leg to knee, open hips and kick. "It was such a strange prayer," I grumble. I'm quite good at it though. Being in harmony with one's angel means compromise around the important things. At least my angel did not insist on watching bardic song performances like some. Why I've heard and long observed that our Temple's master, Lord Tanzen, and his angel must have reached an agreement about horseback riding and stunts.

I never would have thought that things as base as turning a fist into a weapon would become a channel to so many worshippers in a single place. The Soran Temple of Angels draws more curiosity seekers than faithful these days. Ever since the Khasran Lich's defeat, the faithful have been leaving for Khasra. They were either tired of the never-ending back and forth with Morbatten and the dragons, or found themselves pressed upon by the more militant factions within The Temples. I realize I'm lost in reverie and dismiss the class early.

I walk from the amphitheater overlooking the Bay of Ymac into the Temple of Angels. The novelty of seeing our high priests leading classes in Khasran fighting style is no longer strange to me and I harrumph. A guard standing at the doorway between the Temple and amphitheater chuckles and says, "You should try it, old man. It's quite energetic."

I make a fist and shake it Chuuko's face. "Even though the Tanians embrace this, even though our worshippers love it, I'm not taking war to our enemies with just these knuckles. Give me a flameblade and angel wings any day!"

"Truth, Instructor Yussef. Truth," the guard says.

I almost walk into the sparring section but catch myself. The High Priest, our high priest, is sparring with a Tanian. "Who's the dragonlover, Chuuko?" I ask the guard. I almost use the Koran term that would imply more but catch myself. It's an unholy thought and I cannot endure another chastisement from my angel, not after how hard that lecture was. I feel Jun's approval even as she pushes just a tinge of caution about how labels become walls become a vast divide between people. I understand her message: THERE IS MORE AT STAKE HERE THAN PRIDE.

Chuuko answers me with a light tone of voice that suggests he is being careful with his words too. Maybe his angel cautioned him as well. He says, "We received a request from the Queen of Harkenwood a month ago. She asked that we host a Tanian party of three. Three Tanians arrived just after your class started. I thought about sending word, but it's why your class was so poorly attended. I know how that annoys you. My apologies." He points his thumb at them and says, "Best I can tell, they know our fighting styles. The lady now, with Lord Tanzen, is quite good. We think she's a priestess acolyte serving the others, though she is not carrying any royal insignia. The other two are different entirely."

"How so?" I ask. I can sense a hidden humor in Chuuko's words. I'm expecting a joke or a surprise. He does not disappoint.

"Well, that's… Queen Ora and Dar Jeri of the Temple of Tiamat are here. They have a young girl with them…" He paused just enough to prompt me to guess Queen Ora would be a servant to the other two. My eyes bug out. I feel Jun smiling.

I was expecting something but not this. "You mean…"

"Yes, Master Yussef. The Queen, the King's battle priestess, and the Dread Lord Ynt'taris are doing wushu prayers with our High Priest Tanzen." Chuuko cannot contain himself anymore and bursts out laughing. The flat matter-of-fact tone heightens my surprise and I join his laughter.

Usually, Jun would warn me of this. Chuuko's angel must have struck a deal. They do enjoy these moments of ambush, especially if it creates situations like this where my composure is shot and I'm caught gaping and speechless. Thinking it, I feel my angel smiling and laughing with me. It's part of the partnership. I'd be lying if I didn't admit to setting up a few surprises for Jun as well.

"Thank you. Ah, thank you, Chuuko. It has been too serious a day and to walk into this without some levity, thank you a thousand times." I bow to Chuuko and walk onto the sparring floor.

The Tanian queen meets my expectations for a priestess of Tiamat, though I note her beauty with academic cool. I also note that she does not burn with fire or sparkle with rubies and bloodstones like every other Tanian priestess I have ever met. She has an albino-like lack of color in her skin. I wonder if her eyes are white before realizing they have a touch of blue. Only when I squint my eyes do I realize she bears at least three bloodstone rubies cleverly worked into gleaming white metal jewelry. The bloodstones are so small and yet they blaze with power through my closed eyelids. Truly, she is a Tanian Queen.

Lord Tanzen is slowly walking Queen Ora through the steps of some beginner movements. She knows the Tanian forms of these and Tanzen comments on them. "Your former king, Rojo, loved these," Tanzen says as if in a lecture hall. Except for me and a few of the senior-most masters, everyone is eavesdropping and pretending to not see the Dread Lord and Tanians in our temple. Tanzen continues as they pick up the sparring tempo. "In my studies with Dar Rojo, I often noted that he trusted his strength rather than natural grace. Armor will not always protect you. You will not always have a weapon in your hand, or a paladin of dragons as an ally."

Ora moves to strike at the lord priest with her left fist while sweeping her left foot to unbalance him. His right knee twists slightly and barely changes her punch so he can deflect it. She stumbles to the side, her own momentum unbalancing her. Though she quickly recovers, we all note that even she knows Tanzen has completely exposed her heart to attack. He simulates a punch. It has enough force that her goddess armor crackles into being. He pulls his attack well before connecting and smiles at her.

Ora, to her credit, sidesteps back two paces and says, "Pardon me. My training is to defend against any attack. I am unused to your sparring without intent to harm. This is not how we train in Morbatten."

Tanzen bows. "Yes, many of us have trained alongside the dragon priestesses and new battle clerics, such as the late Lord Tembri. Maybe angels watch over his rest." Tanzen points me out as someone who trained with them and I bow.

It's a brief moment of silence while Ora recomposes herself into a strong defensive posture. I'm admiring it when Tanzen compliments her perfect form. The chuckle in his voice sounds friendly. "Lady Ora, that is a good posture for a cleric. To hold this, it empowers you to withstand most attacks without breaking focus. You had a good teacher. Who was it?"

Ora sees he has ended their sparring and bows in the correct Imperic manner, fist clasped in hand before her eyes and upper body inclined straight forward. Ynt'taris walks onto the training surface and answers the high priest. "Our golem master, Sai, instructed Dar Ora. It is good to know Imperius' high priest praises her teaching."

I see how careful and refined Tanzen has become. His body posture remains neutral but, for those of us trained, we see he is at full alert. Jun whispers to me and I hear it in my ear (she must be fascinated by the dragon), "The Tanian ice dragon is a little girl?" Jun has a faint smile in her voice. "Maybe the dragon should follow our rules and…"

I step onto the training mat and bow formally. "Master Tanzen, please, I pray you. Allow me to spar with the Dread Lord Ynt'taris!" It's these little surprises that really get an angel's fascination; the complete and unexpected recklessness of humanity. They see it. They marvel at it. Their perfect design allows it but it is so tempered and cautioned by wisdom that they cannot fathom why for honor, for love, for decorum or tradition, we keep putting ourselves in harm's way over things that, to an angel, are not worth dying for. This is how I know and knew at the beginning that Jun was a divine angel. Ascended angels, drawn from heroic paladin and cleric deaths, have a more practical world view through the veil of what they remember.

Ynt'taris keeps his eyes – the small girl's form throws me off balance – on Lord Tanzen. In perfect Imperic language, a dialect of the Temple language used in long lost Merakor's temples – Ynt'taris says, "I did not come to spar, but if it helps relieve some of the tension here, why not?"

Tanzen bows to the dread lord and steps back. His hand is upright like a blade. When he drops it, our sparring will commence. Tanzen's angel sends condolences and Jun warns me, teasingly, of my advanced age and to be careful, but I have another surprise in store. I'm expecting the formal Tanian combat dance their former king improvised from Imperic training at the Khasran Temple. I show our guest respect and engage in their style. In subtle ways, Ynt'taris lets me know that I am outclassed, overmatched, and a dead man walking were this a real fight. To the dragon's credit, nothing of my age is mentioned and I find my opponent allowing me to look better than needed.

"Dread Lord Ynt'taris," I say in my best draconian. "I am honored and grateful for your kind consideration." I punctuate my words with my best and fastest fist strike. It should land squarely and even Jun blinks her eyes when I miss by a hair's breadth.

Ynt'taris' girl form is precious and beautiful with these otherworldly eyes that make me feel like she isn't even paying attention to me. I can tell my angel is completely jarred by the appearance conflicting with how the dragon must look in reality to an angel that sees only the true nature of things. I send an empathetic hug to Jun while wishing I could see the dragon too.

Somehow, Ynt'taris trips me and lands me square on my back. I could not even feel the grapple; it just happened. I was standing and then I was on my back. A cold spot along my outer shin and along my wrist tell me a judo move defeated me. I spring back up, shaking the cold from my wrist. Jun is upset. Even she did not sense the attack.

Tanzen says, "Point to the ice patriarch. Another point wins."

I do not wait. Knowing all eyes in the Temple are watching, and onlookers are arriving by the minute, - and Jun informs me that scrying has become active in the Temple too, I charge. The dragon-girl-child intercepts my charge in a wheeling arm defense that should redirect my momentum so that I will stumble past and be open to a counter-attack. A well-placed trip would drop me and end our sparring session. This is what I'm counting on and I hold my breath.

Jun does not let me down. Though invisible to all but angels and their companions, Jun's arm is glorious to me and she catches Ynt'taris' movement. I hear the onlookers gasp as the dragon's arm motion is halted by an invisible force. Jun strains and yells out, "Let's see if you're dragon strong in my father's house!"

Time seems to pause and Ynt'taris locks eyes with Jun's five-pace tall form standing over and through my own. The dragon says, "Yes, I am."

Jun wilts. I want to use a different word to describe it, but cannot find one. Even Jun concedes she is wilting. She may have even said, "Errp." It's not a common or angelic sound.

Ynt'taris throws my angel. I am sent tumbling twenty paces off the sparring floor to slide on the polished marble floor. Eventually, I smash into a column and lay there dazed. Jun lays there dazed with me. White feathers rain down around me from damage to Jun's wings.

Tanzen's angel comes over and heals us both. I do not know what the angel's name is, and we do not hear it during the healing prayer. Until sound intrudes in my ears, I did not realize I had suffered a concussion or lost my hearing. Tanzen remains guarded but relaxed. "Two points. Victory to Dread Lord Ynt'taris, Patriarch of Ice, King of Morbatten. Let our records show flawless victory against Instructor Yussef."

He continues. "Yussef will recover and be just fine. We did not realize our Tanian guests are so adept at Imperic techniques. In my own studies with late King Rojo, I found him a genius student but these techniques…"

"Are well known and studied and documented by my brother, Alerius." Ynt'taris slowly turns in a circle and locks gaze with every person in the Temple. "We had hoped to include this in our own martial training back in the time of Dar Tania and the Great Sage Alaura, but we lacked the divine touch a worshipper of Imperius brings to instruction. There was no Imperic like Commander Sean of Pha Rann to guide our people."

When the dragon says Commander Sean I sense a flash of anger from the dragon and my own anger is kindled. My soul wants to scream out, "I will be there for you! I will teach you!" I realize this is a form of dragonterror. That Ynt'taris feels this after nearly two thousand years gives me a new insight into the Tanian dragons: even though they reject the Path of Light and defy the Eye of God, they know that our way is better than what they have pieced together by careful research.

The dragon continues, "The Angel God has our gratitude. Rojo the First spoke glowingly of his time with you all here in the Temple. It is too bad the Temple does not feel the same about Morbatten."

Tanzen looks confused and at a loss for words. He graciously says, "You have only our deepest respect, Lord Dragon." But, the tone of his voice asks the question: *what are we accused of?*

Ynt'taris points to a man in plate armor standing by a column behind the crowd of onlookers. "This one was gifted a blank bloodstone. When we called for unity against Orcus, this one and many of his followers refused to answer our call. Though the Temple of Imperius rose up with High King Andrew, you sheltered this group in open rebellion. Your Temple knew. I do not understand why you would so dishonor yourselves in this matter. The Valley of Bloodstone contained glory for all. Sharing was not an issue when Bomoki's Gate fell. Over a bloodstone, Imperius' holy name is sullied. How would you correct this, Master Tanzen?"

Tanzen looks to where Ynt'taris points but the man is already fleeing. Tanzen snaps his fingers and an angelic command resounds to us all: *Pursue and Capture, combat orders.*

Wings burst from my armor. I see Ceanne rise up already climbing so she can swoop after the runaway. All around us, the paladins of Imperius grow wings and give chase. Combat orders means we can use anything in our arsenal to apprehend our target, even killing him. Maybe the dread lord has made Tanzen that anxious to invoke combat orders when we are not in a clear state of war.

Ceanne is ahead of me and Jun chides me for admiring how the wings and armor accentuate her form. I chuckle. A life of celibacy, an unusual requirement from my angel, has made me hyper-appreciative of the ladies. Jun chides me.

From what I can see and remember, the man we are chasing is an adventurer who frequently contracts with The Temples for work around what the paladins are doing. I do not remember having ever spoken to him, but I know his reputation. Jun fills me in on some other details: two-time veteran of Bloodstone, dropout from clerical training (lacked the dedication required to hold sacred focus in his heart), and he has approximately twenty retainers. From time to time, clerics have joined his parties for especially difficult missions. His name is Demaris. I feel some relief from the dragon's accusation. Demaris is not a member of the Temple of Angels. No doubt Tanzen will investigate the dragon's claims and we will find some excuse for Demaris not reporting to the Valley of Bloodstone. Still, it's odd that a veteran would shirk that. "It's not like Demaris at all, right Jun?"

Jun is trying to get information from the other angels. As I fly after Ceanne, Jun brings me information. Demaris returned from a high profile mission for a Soran patron three years ago and never quite recovered. No one had seen him in a state of active worship or contracting with the Temple since that quest, whatever it was. He would not speak of it. He believed he was cursed but multiple attempts by our clerics yielded nothing. Though his retainers continued to work for us, Demaris did not.

As Jun shares this with me, I wish I could convey this information to Ceanne's angel. He would be able to tell her. It's not telepathy, but it's handy when things are loud and chaotic like this. Maybe Demaris is cursed, I concede to Jun.

Ceanne's angel has yet to reveal himself, and Jun chides me: *It could be a lady like me*. I want Ceanne to win and she is in front. I feel my comrades sweeping in behind us. The younger and faster paladins, with angels driven by a more competitive spirit, will overtake us.

Demaris runs into a garden courtyard, and I know we have him. At Jun's command, vines and roots lash out at his legs and he trips, falling head over heels as bits of armor break free. I flare my wings to block the others from seeing. Ceanne will score her first win. I swear it.

My angel commands the others to stop, and they must. Even though the paladins do not want to, they cannot continue flying without their angels' consent. I drop to the ground and walk out, wings open wide to block the other paladins from seeing. Ceanne can do this.

Ceanne holds a sword pointed at Demaris' throat. He has the right pose of a cornered man who knows he cannot run anymore, but there's something else in his eyes. Jun sees it too. I sprint forward and call out a warning. The paladins behind me charge.

Ceanne looks up with concern at my call and misses seeing the man's form break apart as he changes into a giant brown spider bearing black bands. Spiny legs explode outward from the man, so large the transformation knocks Ceanne backwards. She stumbles and catches herself. For a moment, I see an angelic radiance. Maybe today is the day her angel introduces himself – *herself!* – to us.

My sword sweeps like a scythe at the nearest leg. The monster lifts it up to dodge and then stabs it back down at me. The end of that leg is all hard carapace and spikes dripping with ichor. I block out the vision of the spider's underbelly and spinnerets. It's ugly.

My friends cut in at that leg and quickly amputate it. The spider wheels to face us as webs spray out and coat the Temple's exits to the courtyard. I note that the leg is regenerating. Jun confirms what I know, that there are no records of regenerating and shapeshifting spiders. This is something else. With a blank bloodstone at stake, maybe Demaris is a mage. I wonder. He does not seem like a mage, and I should know that, given his long association and reputation within the Temple.

While my fellow knights form up to corner the spider, I stand back. Jun strengthens my spine and shoulders. I feel tall and strong, like a giant. Jun leans forward and puts her eyes over my eyes and I see.

Our opponent is not Demaris. It's a Red Slaad. I blink. Jun blinks. Neither of us can believe it and we look again. I snap my fingers and the sound echoes back to Lord Tanzen with my message. *Master, a Red Slaad has replaced Demaris. It is cornered in the eastern garden. There are ten of us. We need any and all reinforcements.*

The spider breathes a mist through its biting fangs. The mist is purple and yellow glinting in the sunlight. The paladins shudder when it hits them and I see their angels step forward to heal and augment their strength, their vitality, and to steel their resolve. "My friends, reinforcements are coming! It's a Slaad, a red one. We must defend and buy time against this Embros!"

The veteran knights, the ones who have been around enough to have learned what a Slaad – what an Embros is, immediately fall back. The others, those who were not paying attention in my classes or are too new like Ceanne, press forward. They do not know what an Embros is. They do not… and then, I feel it. Jun fortifies my will as the garden around us cinders to melting glass. The spider sprouts wings and the venom of its breath corrodes the armor of the knights. An infernal chittering sound fills the courtyard and I see my aged hands begin to rot.

I ignore it and Jun ignores it and we are fine. The curse of what the Slaads call 'Set's Dream' cannot harm the faithful. I concede to myself that those possessed of a particularly strong will seem to be okay too, but it has to be luck.

The stones and plants around us are actually melting. If the Tanian records are true, an Embros can affect any reality it sees. This must be an ancient Embros to use the Dream. They're normally so battle-lusted they can barely function like a normal Slaad... unless they are ancient.

True to the Tanian canon, the shifting reality asserts and flows as its gaze shifts around. Even though my hands feel rotten, and my brain cannot believe they are still attached, I draw my holy avenger and call out my prayerful challenge. "Hear me, creature of Set! The faithful stand arrayed against you! You have but one chance – surrender!"

My words strengthen my friends and their forms solidify. Trembling hands, warped and bent by age and gangrene, clutch at swords enwrapped by their angels' fingers. *The flesh is willing but angels are all-powerful*, I remember the old adage and change my mindset to address the angels present. "Chorus of Heaven, hear me! An Embros stands before us and we must fight! Take your mortal vessels and defend!"

Jun swells up in power around me as the Chorus of Heaven obeys. Jun is an Avatar of Command. The stronger my will, the stronger Jun's Command is. The stronger my faith, the more powerful the Command is, much like the Slaad and how it uses Set's Dream to change reality.

To my dismay, it takes time for my will and faith to fully bring Jun into her regal and lordly state. Ceanne, unable to hear me, charges forward. She masterfully slashes at a leg and spins around, using her momentum to cut a semi-circular gash and then pierce through the spider leg.

A single spider eye looks down at her, and she liquefies to gore under Set's Dream. I do not even get to see or hear her scream. She is as unaware of her sudden death as an ant would be against an avalanche. Ceanne was one of my favorite students. Righteous anger kindles in my heart. Jun nods her head and we charge. *We*, for I am in my angel as if armor, and my wings shimmer with Creation's power.

It is my hand that holds my avenging long sword, but it is Jun's hand that amputates a leg and spins razor wings through six more. Jun orders the limbs to not regenerate, "Healing revocation," she states. The fact is clear. The legs do not regenerate and the Slaad spider collapses to one side.

The body's stinger lunges forward and Jun's left wing covers my body to become like a a full body-sized shield against which the poison fang and venom sac impact. The wing shudders but does not move. Waves of chaos pulse over us as eight spider eyes now focus Set's power against me. I feel my faith waver and the shield disintegrates to Jun's plaintive cry. I hear her pain as a chastisement to hold my faith strong. Her wing can only be shield strong as my faith is strong. My guardian's pain shakes me out of my dread fascination and I entrust my faith to her.

Tumbling past the shield, I stab my sword up into the spider's mouth. It should connect. It will strike true. My faith… falls flat as the spider shapeshifts into a multi-headed dragon-like creature. Each dragon has a tiara of eyes encircling its entire head. The spider legs absorb into the body and become new dragon legs. The shapeshifting compensates for the damage and I note a sense of frustration from my foe. We had wounded seven of the eight legs and I note seven fairly severe wounds along the hydra's torso. This has to be a Slaad interpretation of a hydra.

There are so many eyes are now looking everywhere. I can tell what the eyes focus on because, like Ceanne, things liquefy and collapse into rot, even stone. A small squad of angels stands against the Embros. "Attack!" I roar.

We press forward against the hydra. Jun has recovered but I can tell there are lingering effects; the Slaad is fighting Jun for the reality of being wounded; it wants its regeneration powers back. Amidst that dark realization, one of the five dragon-like heads whispers to Jun. The words spill out as emblems that twist and writhe like a mass of snakes. I know they aren't real. Jun knows they cannot touch us, but the words become understanding in our minds. The Slaad is alien to Tehra. Its thoughts are rage and hunger… for Jun. We both feel its hunger for her. This must be what prey feels in the moment it realizes it has been ambushed by a stealthy predator.

Three of the five heads exhale at our group. Two heads remain focused on Jun and me, though I note eyes reinforcing Set's Dream to block anyone in the Temple from reaching us. Expecting fire, we raise shields and brace. Instead, a mass of abyssal insects swarms out of the mouths. When there is no fire, I look up and see my own reflection in a bleeding eye with insectoid wings. It bumps into my face and feels wet. Then, it pops and acid splatters down my face. All around me, my fellow knights scream in pain. I do not scream. I've felt such great pain in my life that this is nothing. The acid burns my eyes and I go blind, but my faith in Jun such that she steps in and lends me her eyes. My world becomes clearer than if I could still see.

The angels react and spin their wings around the group. Where feathers of pure light, razors like Jun's, or of fire touch the insect plague, the bugs burst and gore falls hissing to the molten ground. The smell of cooking flesh now fills the garden.

I know I do not have much time. While Jun assists with clearing the bugs, I use a magic ring on my index finger that makes me invisible and I charge forward. The Slaad can probably see me, but only if it's looking for an invisible paladin. Why would it? Imperius and The Temples have forsworn illusions and cloaking magic for millennia. This is my surprise. I am fascinated by magic, and Jun loves me for it. Tanzen thinks I'm antiquated in my thinking.

I dart under the heads as they spew bugs. Too late, the Slaad sees me and a hydra head lunges down. I slide on the wet ground and cut under the chin of the hydra head and find myself under the shoulder area. The Slaad's radial scars are barely recognizable interwoven in the hydra scales. The center is above my reach, but if I can slay the transformant worm nestled where the Slaad's heart is, I can permanently end this abomination.

I need Jun's height and combat strength. Something else though answers my call and I feel a different angel step into being around us; Jun is focused on staying in alignment with my eyes. "Who are you?" I whisper.

The angel answers, but Ceanne's voice bellows through. "Master Yussef, her name is Retrial!"

Retrial… a second chance, I get it. Her angel brought her back. Retrial is a much stronger angel than Ceanne is a paladin and I smile. "Welcome to The Temples, Divine Retrial." Later, Ceanne and Retrial will select a different name. Jun's first name was Command. This is a common milestone with all paladins. Divine avatars do not really have names. They find it a quaint point of interest that we name everything and everyone. When they get a name, it becomes a point of pride for them.

Retrial throws me like a spear at the radial scar's center. My sword is burning and my heart is pure. The Slaad shapeshifts to avoid my striking a critical blow. Its mass falls away from us until a four-armed giant of reddish brown scales stands nearly fifty paces away from us. It is huge, easily as tall as a frost giant. The unhinged jaw that reaches back nearly to its spine mocks us with razor teeth from which a few more oculus insects wriggle out to attack us. Two of the arms slam into the stone and splash molten rock high into the air at us.

The Embros has lost its focus. This is both good and bad. Good because it means the effects of Set's Dream will lessen. Bad because, if the Tanian stories are true, Red Slaads are beasts of battle. They crave and worship carnage. Embros because of wrath, is how the ancient Sage Alaura and their first priestess Dar Tania described it.

The Embros charges us and just as we brace for impact, it blinks out of being, teleports behind us, and slams into my back with all the momentum of its charge. Like being hit by giant mallet, I let Jun's and my armor take the brunt of the impact. Next thing I know, I'm looking at the molten courtyard from high in the sky. Ceanne and her angel were smashed into a statue's plinth nearly a hundred paces back in the garden. The statue has cracked and shattered. Retrial lets go of Ceanne and puts her gently on the ground. She is fine though Retrial's wings are broken and bleeding.

Jun's wings open to catch me as I'm still rising into the sky. My lower back is shattered and I cannot feel my legs. Jun's concern is touching. I reassure her and say, "I've had worse, my love. My faith and my will to fight remain intact. Let's go show this Embros the true meaning of power!"

I feel her lips touch my hand and imagine her doing a curtsey. "Your wish is my command," I imagine her whispering. We raptor dive towards the Embros. One of my friends is speared through by finger talons the size of a polearm puncturing his chest. His angel lies broken and unresponsive.

Though my legs will not move, Jun's feet become golden talons that we barrel into the Embros just as it is about to feed on the impaled knight.

We tumble with the Slaad. Jun cannot protect me from the slashing claws of the Red. Focused on me, the Embros cannot defend itself from Jun's attack against its eyes. I note there are four and a new one is opening in its chest right in front of my face.

One of those slashing claws punches into my mid-section and spills my innards out through the broken plate of my cuirass. So much pain, but I remain focused on my faith and vision of victory; it is what Jun needs to win, to buy time. Jun releases my sword arm to drive her own fingers into the Red's eyes as her wings slash into the other two. All around us, the remaining angels are attacking the eyes as they open across the Red's body.

I can hear only my heartbeat. It is loud and furious. I'm bleeding to death. I can hear my own death in the rising amplitude of my heart. Tania taught us that even in death, with focus, we can continue to act for a few critical moments. I remember a Dar priestess smirking at me when I was much younger. Dar Niss… her fiery hair looks so distant. "You have forty-five seconds, even without your heart beating, to force action. Make it count."

I still have my heart. The problem is I'm running out of blood for it to pump. Dar Niss taught us that too: Brain Death, she called it. "1…" I count. My fingers curl on my long sword. "2…" I count as I fixate on the eye just opening before me. Another hand rises up before my face as the Embros twists its claw in my mid-section. If I weren't paralyzed and unfeeling from my broken spine, it would really hurt. I see an armored index finger coiled against the thumb. It aims at my head, to flick it off. The eye is watching and I point my sword at it. "3…" and I stab my sword into the radial scar.

The stupid Embros thought I would go for the eye. Jun is crying in agony, because we feel each other's pain, and white razor feathers are falling around the Embros, cutting into its flesh. She orders me to live. "4…"

Our world, in that moment, is perfect. Pain, all is pain, and love in the midst of a heroic battle with the truest love of my life. To die in the arms of my angel, to defeat a foe like this worthy of my life's work and death… I smile and fall, but part of me wonders why my world has grown cold. Why is Jun flinching? "5…"

Something large catches me. Well, it deflects my fall and I slide on now frozen ground. I feel a warm hand touch my face and draconian whispers urge me back to life. The ground trembles all around me and then healing agony pulls my perforated intestines back into my body. Ice glazes my armor together. Fire replaces my lost blood and I scream as searing life floods back into me. My heart is pumping fire and my world is ablaze.

I see my beautiful and perfect death falling away. Maybe it's the dragon magic or something about Tiamat's dominion, but I find I am beyond angry at being pulled back from the beautiful dream of my life's ending.

I feel Jun holding me, but realize I am embraced by the Tanian Queen, Ora. "Go, noble paladin," she says. "Fight. We must know why and how an Embros came to be here."

Her blessing is augmented by the other dragon priestess, Dar Jeri. Her words pulse heated fury into every cell of my body. I recognize the prayer from my studies. The Imperic version of this smooths the world out, makes things easier, and brings a calm focus. The Tanian form is like a dragon breathing directly into my blood. Jun feels my vigor and screams for me to join her. Ora pushes me to my feet and helps me turn to see the fight. My eyes have healed finally and I choke on the carnage. The fighters have all fallen. Their companion avatars are so hurt, I wonder how they still stand, guarding their knights.

Ynt'taris, as a dragon, is smaller than I would have thought but still dwarfs the Red Slaad. Somehow, they are locked in combat and the Embros is not yet defeated. As I watch, it shrugs and ice locking half its body and most of its head shatters free. Only three angels remain and they are trying to attack as opportunities present. One lunges forward and strikes at the Embros as the dragon coils and twists and holds the Slaad for the attack. It looks like the flamesword will cut into Ynt'taris and then suddenly, the dragon's body exposes the Embros for the attack. I see the radial scars shapeshift just enough to prevent a critical attack by the angel. A trailing splash of blood freezing in the air is all I see before the twisting grapple shifts away from me.

The other dragon priestess, Dar Jeri, is moving to clear the blocked entrances. I hear the angels of other paladins and the yells of our own priests wanting to join the fray. How can the Slaad survive the combination of physical and magical attacks by Ynt'taris? Either the Tanian dragons are not as strong as their reputations suggest, or the Slaad is incredibly powerful.

Ynt'taris coils around the Embros and bites one of its arms while breathing ice, or whatever that dragon's breath weapon is. A part of me, my scholarly self, remembers reading something by the great sage Alaura about how Ynt'taris does not breathe as much as he consumes heat energy from a target. The Slaad's arm shatters into a million ice fragments, but I see deep gashes open in the ice patriarch's side as the other three arms claw and dig through the scales to pull flesh out in gaping handfuls.

The Slaad's overly-large mouth bites into the dragon's neck and I wince. The teeth are as big as my long sword. It has to hurt, but I am running to join Jun. Ora's blessing has lit my soul on fire and I want to burn everything down, especially the Slaad. My sword materializes in my hand and I jump with all my might. Mid-air, Jun wraps me in her wings and my leap takes flight.

Tanzen's angel and Lord Tanzen cannot be distinguished. They are one and the same and our master is glorious as he runs nimbly along the dragon and Embros' battle. His mace pulverizes one of the Slaad's eyes! He jumps free of counterattack. The other angels begin attacking with magic, not wanting to risk their mortal friends in close combat when a real dragon is willing to engage the front line.

"Jun, are we going to let the Tanian dragon take our foe?" I imagine her screaming, "No!" and we dive at the Embros. I scream out in draconian, "Ynt'taris, pull your head back in 3, 2, 1..."

The dragon does so and my body, my sword, my angel spears the Embros through its head, cutting clear through and exploding out the backside. It feels victorious but I continue to hear combat.

When I wipe the gore and brain matter from my eyes, I see a headless Embros continuing to fight. Eyes continue to open across its body. "Jun, how can it continue fighting?" I whisper this out loud thinking no one can hear me. An image of a cockroach flashes in my mind, but I'm already throwing us back into the assault on the Embros. Against that image, I have an epiphany. The Slaad's consciousness is not the brain. It's the source of the infection in the radial. It has to be.

My flying leap and driving sword point are perfectly aligned with the Embros' back. I can feel another mighty hit in my bones but instead, I end up cartwheeling and spinning, trying to avoid stabbing the dragon. I feel reality shift all around me as the Embros looks back at me and Jun, except I see myself standing on the ground amidst the dragon's body and claws.

The other paladins hesitate as they see two of me, one of the mes (the real one) appears to be attacking the ice dragon. The other is floating in the air with angel wings where Jun and I began our dive. The Slaad switched places with me. It looks bad. Jun is screaming at the other angels, but I notice the Embros' "angel" is too. How does a Slaad know the divine speech of Heaven?

Thankfully, Ynt'taris and the Tanians are completely unaffected. For one, the Embros cannot see the priestesses who are outside its field of vision. And two, dragonterror seems to affect Slaads. Ynt'taris opens his mouth and a white light splintered by glacier blue spears up at the Embros. Jun and I, Tanzen, and the Tanians remain strong as a primordial fear and awe grips our bones. To me, it feels like a zephyr on a hot summer day and I realize: Ynt'taris considers me an ally. Ceanne and the newer paladins, fall to the ground in fetal positions. One tries to run away, but his angel stops and holds him.

The Embros-as-me teleports and misses the breath weapon attack. Apparently, the ice dragon *can* breathe ice, I note. The Embros teleports and reappears behind Queen Ora, appearing like her now. Ynt'taris does not miss a beat. His ice lance swings to follow the Slaad's teleport and leaves a freezing trail of enthalpic destruction towards Ora.

The real Ora catches it in her hand. The Embros-as-Ora mimics her. I've never seen an ice priestess. It makes sense they might have different abilities than the Tanian fire priestesses. Those are all seduction and beautiful rage. Ora is cool and serene as the ice breath strikes her hand. Somehow, she holds it… and I hear it: draconian rumbling. Ynt'taris is singing spellsongs with a Merakoran inflection I have never heard before. Ora is answering him though the soprano of her voice is drowned by crystalline ice sounds.

The Embros looks at its own hand and shrugs. She is catching all the energy. It reveals her as the real priestess. Standing so close to her, the Slaad attacks. Ora remains focused and Tanzen intercepts and blocks slashing claws just a finger from the priestess' neck. I can see her goddess armor scintillate under Tanzen's fists. In human form, the Slaad cannot use its bulk though it is clearly strong enough to defy Tanzen. I am so proud of our Grand Master as his flurry of fist and kick attacks drives the monster back a few steps.

Now, another rumbling fills the garden and Dar Jeri shapeshifts into a gold dragon. I've seen Oranstakar the Golden Sage many times. I've seen artist renditions of gold dragons. Jeri is definitely a gold dragon. In the space between her radiant scales, I see dark ember fire and it reminds me of the Tanian script for Tiamat. A gold dragon who serves Tiamat, I marvel. We knew. I knew, of course, that the king's battle priestess is a converted gold. Tanians are obsessed with preaching Tiamat to the metallic dragons.

I go back into my beautiful rage. Jeri's neck snaps forward and grabs the Embros by its shoulder. There is a blood mist and then yellow fire when she throws the Embros into the air. As it rolls and twists into the sky, Jeri continues baptizing it in flame.

Ora captures the last bit of Ynt'taris' breath weapon in her hand into a tiny sphere of white clasped in her fingers. It is snowing around her now. More and more reinforcements are arriving through the spider webs, but their participation is hindered by the Temple's size. We have a quiet moment where, in between the crackling ice and roar of the dragon's fire, I wonder what to do next. We are hurting the monster, but it still has so much fight in it.

I remember reading a long-ago note by Alaura. It said that the Dragon King Alerius shied away from confronting a Blue Slaad, a step weaker than a Red, without his court. I've seen the regeneration and teleportation abilities. The shapeshifting and reality bending by themselves would have made me take caution. An Embros… and there is not a court of Tanian eldar dragons here. I have to concede that we might be overmatched.

The battle is entering a new phase. We all sense it. Jun and I look for an opening as the Embros comes to a halt in the air high above us. Smoke blows away in the wind. Burning skin sloughs off and I know the Slaad is regenerating. "What will it be?" I wonder. "Teleport, or…"

The Slaad seems to stand high above us. Before me, the ice and fire dragons are preparing to leap into the sky. Ora, the Queen of Tania, stands like a goddess holding a pulsating sphere of white light in her hand. It is snowing around that sphere. I can still hear the draconian rumbling between the three of them and regret I did not study it more.

"Something else," I confirm to myself as a black slice opens in the sky, and then another. Three more rip open and I know we are doomed. Too many of our forces are still in Bloodstone. The Temples are not necessarily well-fortified even though we have a few heroes around at all times, like Lord Tanzen. The Embros will gate in more Slaads. I cannot even tell how badly we've wounded it. More of this and I imagine Taysor crisping away to ash in the flame of war… spawned by just one of these monsters.

Jun cautions me against despair as the dark portals shimmer with color and things begin to come through. I shake and try to hold onto her caution; we've been in bad situations before. We must endure even though part of me, at last, appreciates how Merakor might have fallen the way it did.

To my right side, Ora begins praying in draconian. Unlike her strange song with the white dragon, this time her song is loud and suggests heroic deeds. Her prayer is a battle hymn and it conjures images to my mind of fences, barriers, and walls. The white globe in her hand seems to power what happens next. The black portals freeze and begin to fall. Limbs, monstrous faces, whatever is coming through them is frozen. I can imagine them shattering. One falls on the roof of the Lightist Temple, and, to my great satisfaction, it shatters just like glass. I see parts of gated demons trapped in ice shatter just as surely as if they were ice too. With smug satisfaction, June chides me to not lose hope so easily.

The Embros glares at Ora and I know what's going to happen. Co-opting Jun's Voice of Command, I call out. "Rally around the Queen! Defend her! She is preventing the monster from gating in allies."

As those of us on the ground move to surround Ora, the two dragons leap into the sky. I'm expecting a ponderous and slow ascent. The leap carries the ice dragon almost to our Temple spire, and then wings open and he flies at the Slaad above him, accelerating in a straight upwards line, like a spear made of pure dragon. Another snippet from Sage Alaura comes to mind: *They fly by will and magic, not like a bird.*

The Slaad welcomes the dragons as fire and ice reach out to it. At the last instant, the Slaad vanishes. Around Ora, we are wary but also caught off guard when the Embros appears right in front of Ora for just a moment. Swirling globules of fire hang in the air and I count seven total. "Fireballs!" I yell. "Paladins, do your thing!"

The closest globule of fire is in front of her face. My holy avenger and a prayer to defeat evil magic on my lips slices the fire. To Ora's credit, she does not flinch at all. The fire splits in half and vanishes against my divine protections. My fellows dispatch the other flames too and it seems too easy.

My suspicion fires Jun's and she lends me her eyes again. The Slaad did teleport in, but he took Ora with him. We defeated illusions spawned by Set's Dream. The two are standing atop the Imperic Temple, alone. Ora retains her focus on preventing gates. She is bleeding. Her aura shows us how terrified she is. "Jun, show the dragons." She does so with a question as to whether a creature of Hell will understand an angel.

Ynt'taris' head whips in that direction and I understand. Not only is Ora terrified, but whatever Jun saw has now terrified Ynt'taris. I refocus and see something in the Slaad's hand near Ora's heart. Her bodice is ripped open. Though her goddess armor is resisting, the Slaad is grinding its hand against the goddess armor and not letting her go with its other arms. There is a darkness in the Slaad's hand pressing against Ora's breast. Arms hold her legs by her thighs and another pressing against her back squeezing her arms to her sides. The titanic Embros compared to tiny Ora made it hard for me to see, but now I do: all of the Slaad's eyes are focused on the goddess armor over her heart… where the Slaad has its radial infection. My heart begins to drop and I pray for the Tanian Queen.

Fear like I have never felt before hammers into my body. It is so dire I do not recognize it as fear. Jun gives it a name: *dragonterror*. In naming it, I feel her succumb to fear with wonderment. I imagine her groan out, "So this is primal fear?"

We both fall to the ground like empty sacks. My fingers tingle and go numb as my sword falls. Jun tries to grab it for me and can barely wiggle it. Try as I might, I cannot even make a fist. I feel Jun's resignation that this eldar dragon overpowers even her divine might. The city must have gone quiet too; all I can hear is my racing heartbeat. I see a flock of birds, paralyzed in fear... they all begin to fall. The clouds in the sky, the sun light, the burning ash, it all seems to stop. Only Ynt'taris moves.

The Embros moves as well, but slower than the dragon, resisting the time freeze somehow. All around, all I hear is draconian and the rushing of many winds, or water. Three of its claws positioned before her heart are pressing in. All of its eyes are starring at that spot. I imagine rays of magic eroding the goddess armor and, despite our theological differences, I pray for the Tanian Queen.

Ora's goddess armor is cracking. She remains focused on preventing gates, which continue to open all around. I hear the Embros exult, "Yeeeeessssssss..." as her armor at last splits. What happens next is confusing to me.

Ynt'taris spears her on his claw through her head into her torso and tears her free of the Embros. A feeling of sadness and apology to her, and I know it, to all of us weighs us down with the heaviness of regret. I see a metaphor of a Spear and Shield, but they are not yet ready. As the dragon clears the Embros, I see the monster gripping one of her legs and bloodied gown as it claws at the dragon. The attack is too slow to connect. I expect the dragon to wheel back and exact vengeance. Instead, Ynt'taris heads south towards the Shield Mountains and Morbatten with dripping gore clutched in its left claw. I blink in slow motion. Did the dragon just retreat? My mind cannot process it. What was happening to Ora that Ynt'taris just killed her?

The Embros begins moving faster as the flow of Time reasserts itself. Falling birds catch themselves. The blood mist of Ora's death hanging in the air, at last falls. Jeri's fire strikes the monster. Lord Tanzen grapples the creature from behind. Jun and I grab my sword which bursts aflame again.

The image of Ora's violent death at her master's hand does not sit well with me. I'm too far from the Embros to matter right now. Jun form is wavering as is my faith. There has to be a way to win. This time, I chastise Jun to not lose hope in me. "We will win," I grit my teeth and say to her.

I begin replaying everything through in my mind. Jun tries to help but still sounds despondent. "Stay strong, my love," I whisper to her. "The dragon had a focus in coming her, he must have. They know more about these creatures than anyone."

It comes to me: the bloodstone. This guy Demaris had a blanked bloodstone, that is, one not marked by Tania. That's why it wasn't detonated. Our Temple was focused on the war against Bomoki and Orcus. A small contract adventurer would be easily missed. He probably just walked out or hid somewhere. I remember something then. No one had seen Demaris in some time. And, Slaads do not just show up in the Isles. The two events and the blanked bloodstone have to be connected. I feel a glimmer of hope. This strengthens Jun and I feel her rekindled resolve flow into me, lending my old bones strength.

I call out to the Imperics around me, "I'd love to stay and watch Master Tanzen best this foul thing, but if you'd like to contribute in a different tack, I need volunteers."

Ceanne jumps forward, as does a priest. It's Ian, the priest from my class, the one who had not been paying attention. I can see the hollow look of someone in shock from too much violence. Ceanne looks angry. "I can use your anger,

Ceanne. Priest Ian, you should tend to the wounded on this battlefield. Ceanne and I will go."

He nods and turns to seek out something to do. He flinches whenever a blast of magic detonates atop the Temple building. The strong columns, wrapped in centuries of enchantment, are beginning to crack. Our Temple may not survive.

More hope arrives and I am not at all surprised to see the Cuthberics fall on the Embros. Their formation, born on divine wings, hits the Embros like a spear point. I laugh when I notice their Valley of Bloodstone insignia for the Nineteenth Legion. They must have teleported in when word of an Embros reached them. The tangle of Cutbheric paladins, one of their mages, Tanzen, and the Tanian gold dragon... I wish I could sketch this and carry this vision to the rest of the world.

"Come Ceanne, we need to investigate some things. We run." I touch her and my prayer invigorates our muscles and breathing. We sprint into the Temple. All around us, acolytes and worshippers are recovering from the dragonterror unleashed by the Ice Patriarch.

I find my target: Demaris' quarters. It lies in a quarter of the Temple not visited or tended by Imperius because it serves as a barracks for those working with us. I kick the door open and am disappointed to see what I see. Dead, mangled bodies lie everywhere. Some have been dead for too many days to guess. Unlike normal death, these bodies are desiccated.

Jun and Retrial must be talking, as I am eventually compelled forward to a dead female mage. I flip her over and find her still beating heart clutched in her hands. I jump back and discard my gauntlets. Chaos has touched her. A radial scab is growing outwards from the hole in her ribcage, and I get it. This is what the Red was trying to do to Ora. Same place over her rib cage, and something dark enough to crack goddess armor.

Teeth are growing in the flesh around her shattered breastbone. I gag and nearly vomit when I see something moving in her skin below her swollen abdomen. I had thought it normal corpse decay. Not so, she is pregnant, alive somehow.

"Angels save us," Ceanne prays.

Jun is weeping at the oppressive darkness and evil stink in the room. I chastise her gently to keep her hope and faith in me strong. I call out, "Demaris, what did you get yourself into? Jun, I need your eyes."

She leans forward so I can see through her eyes. I look around for anything hidden, and nearly miss what is so obvious. The bloodstone is in the mage's heart. My gauntlets are starting to warp just from touching the corpse. The leather is turning pink as flesh begins to grow along it. "Ceanne, do not touch anything." I have a few moments before my gloves will begin infecting me.

I snap my fingers. "Master Tenison, knights of Imperius, High King Andrew, Order of Cuthbert, Order of Pha Rannic Literals and Pragmatists. The Temple of Imperius is desecrated by Chaos Spawn, early stages. This is Instructor Marshall Yussef. On my command, and for all our sakes, quarantine and prepare to purge the Temple of Angels, its grounds, and anyone in this Temple. I pray for us all. I pray for Taysor that there are none infected but walking in our fair land."

At my snap, my message flies on angel wings with a vision of what I am seeing in this room to these people. I know the reaction will be sorrow, but action will be immediate, swift in its mercy, and brutal in its requirements.

I turn back to the room. Igniting my avenging sword in fire, I stab it into the heart and feel the bloodstone. Something serpentine moves in the mage's chest cavity. "Ceanne, be on guard. That is a Slaadi worm, it may attack us. Jun, we must burn this chamber with fire if we are attacked. I need to get this stone so we can figure out how and what else came through with the Embros. What is its enchantments?"

Jun wreathes my form in fire. Retrial watches and nods. Touching Jun, Retrial gifts Ceanne similar divine protection. I twist and work my sword in the heart, but the heart is not pliable. It resists like a stone vise. "I'm going to have to use my hands." I remove my nearly useless gauntlets. Teeth are beginning to grow around the palm where I touched the mage.

"No," Jun says. Her voice is real. "No, you must not."

"I must," I insist. "What if there are other Slaads, or this stone summons them? We have to know. What happened to Demaris, the real Demaris? These bodies have been here too long, undetected. It seems the real Demaris may have been replaced at least two years ago or longer. How many more might die if we do not learn all that we can? Think about it Jun," and I flex my hand while eyeing the still pumping organ below my sword. "A Slaad has been in our Temple for all that time! How?"

Jun touches me and I feel her warm hand. The metallic sheen of her skin is beautiful. A tear falls from her eye and she wipes it on my hand. "So heroic, my handsome knight. Yussef, your courage inspires Heaven. Do this thing, that all might live."

If I think too much, I'll never do it. I shove my bare fingers through the cut. I feel the bloodstone. It's as large as an apple. By the time I wrap my fingers around it, I can feel Chaos in my own flesh. Jun is sobbing for me, "No no no…"

I rip the bloodstone free. It looks wrong. Black inclusions darken what should look like crimson liquid. The mage's belly spasms. We do not have much time. I tear Ceanne's cloak from her armor and wrap my hand and the stone in it. Before anyone might react, I bring my sword down on my forearm. "For the greater good," I grunt. Jun tries to stop me. Retrial tries to stop me. Ceanne has that look now, like Priest Ian, and I know this will become part of her nightmares.

"For the greater good," I whisper as I cradle the bloodied stump to my other hand. "I only held it for a few seconds. Jun, look and tell me if I am free of Chaos. Did I remove it in time?" My vision is swimming, but something new is birthing next to us. "Hurry, we must fight now."

Jun's relief tells me I will be okay. I throw my long sword across the room. It too is infested with Chaos, with Set's corruption. The shining metal has split in several places. I cannot tell if mouths or eyes will appear. I close my eyes and envision a long sword in my left hand. Burning heat there tells me my prayers are answered.

Revelation floods my mind as I hear a loud shout from the Supreme Commander of the Cuthberics: TEMPLE IS SECURED. BATTLE RAGES AGAINST THE RED. SCRYING SHOWS YOUR SORE TRIAL AND WE BLESS YOUR SACRIFICE. YUSSEF, PROCEED WITH THE BLESSINGS OF ALL.

Cuthberics are not subtle in their revelatory communications. The message is distracting and I realize I miss the former Master of the Cuthberic Order. Golcir was at least polite.

I bow my head and say prayerfully, "My friends, Heaven blesses us. Join your faith to me, your blades to mine, your souls to my heart." Jun does not want to. This is a suicide pact. I may not survive. Humans do not usually survive combining with divine servants. "By my command," I whisper. The Angel of Command must abide by my righteous desires. "For the greater good."

The angels join me and I Ceanne's touch. I will miss her.

Strength, focus, power, and resolve begin burning my mind and boiling my insides. I drive my firesword into the chest cavity. My sword is joined by three more that whirl and spin like phantoms around my own pillar of blade.

I feel something trying to escape, but it cannot dodge four swords. I twist and angle and feel it, whatever it is, die. Then, while I feel myself ascending towards Heaven, I drag my blade through the torso towards the feet. The pelvis does not even slow my blade. Something is dragging itself into the world, and I kill it before it births. I cannot see the real world. My eyes see only white. I understand the world by revelation and my blade bisects whatever creature the mage held in her body.

* * *

"What is your angel's name?" the paladin asks Ceanne.

"She is the Angel of Retrial." Ceanne bears an emblem on her armor denoting bravery and a Righteous Feat. "She is Retrial but I am coming to think of her as Naomi."

The paladin sits down by her. "Naomi, that's a lovely name. May I ask how you know that is her name? I just barely found my angel."

Ceanne leans back and smiles at the young knight. "Naomi was the name of my daughter long before I was called to the Chorus of Heaven. She died very young and I always wanted a second chance. It never worked out for me. Retrial loves the name, and its symbolism in my life. What does your angel do?"

The paladin smiles. "He says he is the Angel of Instruction and I am to call him Teacher."

Ceanne's eyes open wide and she begins laughing as I show her angel, Naomi, my arm stump. Apparently, even in ascension to Imperius, Set's Infection cannot be healed. Ceanne taps the Righteous Feat token on her armor. "Come with me. I want to tell you a story about your Angel of Instruction. I do believe he might be an ascended, rather than divine one. You know the difference, right?"

My ally jumps to his feet. He is awestricken – maybe infatuated too - with Ceanne even though she is fifteen years older. "Where are we going?"

She replies, "To the Red Monument, to where many of us earned our Righteous Feat. Your angel will enjoy this. Come."

She takes his hand and they run. Naomi takes my good hand. We walk with purpose down the hallway of melted stone, now pinned with remembrances of those who died in this battle. This is my favorite story. This is my life.

I am an angel.

The End

I hope you enjoyed it! If you subscribe to my newsletter you will receive short stories like this for free as regular serial publications available as PDF and MOBI files. The goal of this and all my writing is to bring to light the world of the Forsaken Isles, its gods and heroes, and the stories it contains through different lenses. This one focused on the gods of Creation. Others will focus on Chaos and Warp.

To learn more, check out my website, which has a breadth of detail and content about how Creation, Chaos, and Warp drive the pantheon, religions, and magic of the Forsaken Isles. I'd love to hear from you as well.

Subscribe here: http://forsakenisles.com/contact/ to get other short stories like this for free.

Reviews matter. If you enjoyed this, please consider leaving a 5-star review on Amazon and Goodreads. Thank you so much!

If you have specific questions, you can visit www.forsakenisles.com or my Facebook author page at www.facebook.com/forsakenisles and I would love to hear from you.

www.ingramcontent.com/pod-product-compliance
Lightning Source LLC
Chambersburg PA
CBHW021036130626
46552CB00005B/1867